THE LONG WHITE SICKNESS

a novel by

Cecelia Frey

[handwritten inscription:] Hector: fellow writer wordsmith friend. Hope you find something worthwhile between 'This' + 'Riviera'

Inanna poetry & fiction series

INANNA PUBLICATIONS AND EDUCATION INC.
TORONTO, CANADA

Canada Council **Conseil des Arts**
for the Arts **du Canada**

We gratefully acknowledge the support of the Canada Council for the Arts and the Ontario Arts Council for our publishing program. We also acknowledge the financial support of the Ontario Media Development Organization.

We are also grateful for the support received from an Anonymous Fund at The Calgary Foundation.

Library and Archives Canada Cataloguing in Publication

Frey, Cecelia, author
    The long white sickness / Cecelia Frey.

(Inanna poetry and fiction series)
Issued in print and electronic formats.
ISBN 978-1-926708-90-4 (bound). – ISBN 978-1-926708-91-1 (pdf)

I. Title. II. Series: Inanna poetry and fiction series

PS8561.R48L55 2013   C813'.54   C2013-902587-1
                                              C2013-902588-X

Printed and bound in Canada

Inanna Publications and Education Inc.
210 Founders College, York University
4700 Keele Street, Toronto, Ontario, Canada M3J 1P3
Telephone: (416) 736-5356 Fax: (416) 736-5765
Email: inanna.publications@inanna.ca Website: www.inanna.ca

for the poets

Man's creative struggle, his search for wisdom and truth, is a love story.

—Iris Murdoch, *The Black Prince*

PROLOGUE

THIS IS MY OFFICIAL AUTOBIOGRAPHY, a scorching tale of desire and betrayal. A deeper reading, however, suggests that it is more exactly a story about being in love, a fool's story of too much heart and not enough head.

"Are you kidding? You don't have a heart."

Who said that? A husband? A child? I must slam the door on these intruding voices.

Whichever way you choose to read it, this confession – for all autobiography is confession, an assuaging of guilt, a plea for absolution – is meant to bear witness to the events narrated within, events which centre around an experience so bizarre that divine intervention seems the only logical explanation. That such an uncanny string of occurrences happened to me at the *end* of an otherwise ordinary life, makes that life no less worthy of documentation. Besides, is anyone's life ordinary? Those whose lives seem so on the surface may have intense inner existences. And is that not, after all, where the real life is lived?

Why, dear reader, you well may ask, am I writing an autobiography? Certainly not for fame and fortune, two terms which have become meaningless for me, although at one time they would have meant the world. But it is too late for that. What good are fame and fortune in the afterlife, if there is one? And if there isn't, the point is even more strongly made. All I care about now is the return of those I have loved...

"When have you ever loved anybody but yourself?" Okay. I know that voice. Lara, my beautiful child, lost to a nutso weirdo religious cult in California and, before that, inquisitor supreme of the *materfamilias*.

As I was saying ... the return of those I have loved. But that is not likely to happen, for they have turned into fictions, airy nothings drifting further and further into the past.

"The trouble with you," my first husband's voice comes in loud and clear. Gully was the one who was always telling me what the trouble with me was. "The trouble with you, you live backward instead of forward."

So, is it anybody's business if I want to compost the past? It was my second husband, actually the nicest one, who made scathing comments about what he called my 'junk.' He was referring to my piles of notes and poetry scribblings, without which my attempts at writing would have been even more dismal than they were. When he visits with his new wife and our son, he invariably comments favourably on my present arrangement, how tidy it is. I nod and smile. I do not tell him about the boxes in the storage room beneath Schmidt, nor in my cupboards, nor under the beds. I especially do not tell him about the one labelled 'one-armed bandit.'

"The past is history." Aunt Olive's voice crackles out of a smoke haze like short-wave radio traveling across the Atlantic. My grandfather used to get messages from all around the world that way. In the middle of the night, I'd wake and hear static and little beep beeps. I'd get out of my warm bed and follow the sound to the downstairs living room where he sat in the dark, a green glow from the dial the only light. Together we would listen to those disembodied voices with their mysterious messages.

"The past is a narrative you have to put together to give life meaning," I insist.

"Forget it." It's one of Aunt Olive's favourite phrases. "Life is a crap shoot. Stop beating your head against a wall."

Tough old Aunt Olive, my favourite aunt, my only aunt, the rest of them having died off. Aunt Olive to whom I promised the quintessential prairie novel. I have let her down, just as I have let down so many others. This confession will be my *mea culpa* statement to all those I have betrayed for a man, not even a man, but the dream of a man.

In response I hear Lara's snort of disdain. "Oh yes, it's going to be all about you as usual." She doesn't understand. One's children never do. For understanding it is best to rely on the kindness of strangers. And perhaps that is another reason for this chronicle – that it will find out there in the cold world a few sympathetic souls.

Perhaps too, quite simply, there is a time for the writing of memoirs. The best time, of course, would be after death. Then one could properly sort out what happened, the moment of death itself completing the pattern. Failing that, the next best time would be as close to the Big Event as possible. The end of life quite naturally lends itself to recollection and reflection, sometimes in tranquillity, sometimes in anguish. It is only in advanced age that we begin to see the pattern dictated by our pursuits, and without understanding this pattern, it seems to me that any attempt at figuring it all out and coming to any sort of self-knowledge must necessarily be compromised. Certainly, although possibly I'm a slow learner, it was not until recently that I began to understand the pattern in my life or even that there was one. Yet, when I look back with some perspective from this distance, I can see that even the most mind-stunning entrances and exits were merely part of this pattern and that any attempt to act against the pattern is sure to be met with failure. I can see that it might have been predicted at the beginning that my life would end with the words of the account that follows. This is the story of those intrusions which formed the pattern of my life, the one-armed bandit who stole my heart, others less welcome, others downright upsetting.

"Enough with the philosophical bullshit! Do you think anyone *cares*?" Gully Jillson, the superego on steroids. Is it because he was the first that his voice so often intrudes? I don't hear the last one at all. The middle one, the one on the ranch in the Foothills, I speak with often because of our youngest son, but I don't remember much of what he said during fifteen years of marriage.

But to ignore Gully, this writing, then, is inevitable. The time has arrived. Apart from this documentation, the work of my life is finished. My poems were finished ten years ago, the last betrayal of my obsession. After that, I no longer had the heart for poetry. My fictions have been attempted and failed. My children are grown up, physically at least. I am no longer necessary to anyone. I do not anticipate that anything new or surprising will happen. I have time to retrieve and ponder.

Retrieve what? might be the next question. What does a failed writer in an obscure northern city have to say that will be of interest to the general public or even to an elitist few? Perhaps the answer is *nothing*. At one time the very fact of my age might have given me license to jot down a few wise epithets, a few pithy pieces of advice. The myth of the old crone, the female visionary, may still be revered in some cultures. Unfortunately, ours is not one of them. Alas, aged women in our society are perceived as smelly old bags of skin, wrinkled and unlovely.

"Get real." There's Aunt Olive again. "You're still a young squirt. Wait'll you're my age." But Aunt Olive doesn't feel old. There's the difference.

And Lara. "Blubber and snivel. You're always complaining about something."

True, Lara. But that doesn't mean any one listens.

Writing an autobiography circumvents the problem of an ear to listen. A writer always writes with an audience in mind, which audience gives the writer permission to speak, no matter that the words may be inconsequential, no matter that the audience may be fabricated. Without an audience, the pretence of an audience, all is silence. A woman in my building starved to death yearning for a lover on horseback. When they found her – Schmidt called in the authorities when another tenant noticed a smell in the corridor – her body was emaciated and swiftly decomposing. She lived alone and seldom came out. We forgot that she was there. No ear heard the sounds that she made, in life or in death.

To counter that sort of thing, by writing I have a voice. By writing, I give myself permission to have a voice. The attempt is made.

On a more practical level, I write to set the record straight. I am the only one who can relate the events narrated herein with truth, the only one who can testify for the defence against another's fabrication of lies. I am the only one who witnessed the bizarre circus that paraded in and out of my apartment looking for the prized relic as if it were the Holy Grail, which I suppose, in a way, it was. Like most writers, I could not tolerate people who knocked on my door without an invitation. These interruptions were even less tolerable when the interrupters came, not to see me, but in search of the Head. But I'm getting ahead of myself.

My story takes place in a high-rise condominium complex that included a sports facility, a tanning salon, a restaurant, a hair salon, a Shoppers Drug Mart, and a few small shops displaying high class merchandise that might be of interest to a tourist – Hudson Bay sweaters, Eskimo soap stone carvings, T-shirts with imprints of maple leaves and beavers, red-coated RCMP figures mounted on stalwart steeds. Many apartments in our building were let on a time-share basis, thus a variety of strangers were constantly coming and going, the proof of their brief habitation their names written in the book kept by Schmidt at the front desk – year after year she would file these documents in a storeroom for the auditor. However, the top three floors were reserved specifically for permanent or semi-permanent guests. I had been a guest for seven years, since my last husband fell off a mountain, which was a great disappointment, since I'd been looking forward to an old age of companionship and travel. Before that ... well, everything you need to know will be related quite naturally as events unfold.

It occurs to me, however, that at this point, a few words about myself might be appropriate, a biographical note, so to speak. I am a female of a certain age, as the French put it, with a Ph.D. in Medieval literature. *Everyone* has a Ph.D. nowadays, that's hardly different, but I tell this because it may reveal my fatal flaw, as manifest in my choice of subject. One of my husbands – the Foothills rancher who gave up on me and married a local rodeo queen – instigated a major shouting match, one of those that married couples seem prone to, that start from nothing and build into awesome proportions, by accusing me of intelligence. He said it was my strong point. I said I thought my strong point was my ability to love but he shouted me down. My strong point was my fatal flaw, he said, because it was – and here I can see the veins bulging in his forehead – a *wrong* intelligence, a *wrong* mind, a *wrong* way of thinking. He was wrong. He mistook intelligence for brooding thoughtfulness. Anyway, I was born that way, with a furrow between my brows, and could do nothing about it. But he thought I could.

In what follows, please think of me as plain Constance. What does the surname matter? Whichever name I give, either that of husbands or fathers, would refer to the patriarch. I was born in the country of farming stock, which likely contributed to the furrow. I grew up in the north and migrated to southern Alberta where I have lived off and on ever since, the off part being not so much shifting abodes as shifting my body in extensive travelling. I married, raised a family, and wrote a dissertation that I will not name since most of the words in the title even I now find incomprehensible. Suffice to say, it left me totally unprepared for the labour market and real life but adequately prepared for the task of teaching writing classes at a junior college. As a second profession, I drifted into writing, mostly freelance material, and was published in a diverse list of publications from architectural design glossies to zoological journals. As for my real writing, my poetry, my life's oeuvre, I continued it over the years, working my craft and sullen art, as well put by Dylan Thomas, if not in the still night, during those frantic interludes when I could crowd it into the few empty slots in my schedule, for at that time I was still a ranch wife and mother with all that entails, the details of which I will not bore the reader with. To paraphrase another poet, Leonard Cohen, I gave my writing a slice of my life. Obviously, the slice was not large enough, as I managed to squeeze out a mere half dozen slim volumes of poetry, none of which sold more than a couple of hundred copies. Let us say that my audience was small but discerning.

In what follows, I will try to be accurate. Now I wish I had kept a diary. But it would have been dull. A few marriages, several children, the ups and downs of the TSX Composite. Times of planting and foaling, ski trips, PTA meetings, literary readings – it all sloshes around in my mind along with the great dinners and wines shared with friends. I do, however, remember with preciseness the end. It was not that long ago.

I have spent considerable time contemplating where to begin. Some autobiographers start with the moment of their birth and then proceed in orderly chronological fashion. Others start with the end and recount their past history in a series of flashbacks. Still others pinpoint some dramatic moment, some thematically correct crisis, and fan out from there.

After much thought and measured deliberation, since, as I have said, things became more interesting at the end, I have decided to start with my suicide.

1.

A FLAP OF WIND SLAMMED ME toward the precipice, the first assault of gusts through the Gap at the summit. I dug in my skis and poles. I would have to travel under the wind or slip through spaces between bursts. Otherwise, the force could blind me in a swirl of impenetrable white, spin me around directionless and hurl me to my doom. At the least, it would blow me backwards, slowing me to a snail's pace. And I was already late for my death.

On the other hand, blowing snow would cover my tracks and confuse searchers. There would be searchers. I planned it that way. I left my old clunker in the deserted parking lot at the start of the run. Eventually someone would notice it piling up with snow and alert the RCMP, but that could take several days. To give myself more breathing space, I had removed the registration papers. I thought of burying the license plate in the snow where it wouldn't be found until spring, but it seemed unnecessary. The Ice River run was mostly abandoned during current weather conditions, which was one reason for my choice. Another was that it was not impossible. It was reasonable for me to have attempted.

The wind had stopped me close to the cliff edge rising up from the river valley. I looked up at the lowering sky. Because of twenty centimetres of new snow, it had taken me too long to get this far. I had tired too soon. I was not the skier I used to be. Those brilliant winters of skiing with my last husband in Norway were nearly a decade ago. Oh, for that husband at a time like this. He was a master at breaking trail. The way he could manoeuvre through all that white was sheer poetry. Both of my real husbands were profound skiers.

Well, Gully was real, too, in the sense that we were really married, but he was a writer, so that hardly counts. Even before the official ceremony, he always had an eye out for some female who could turn his crank and get his writing engine going. He called it pursuing his Muse. Being young and naive, I believed him. In contrast, my second husband was such a nice man, in spite of the fact that he was wrong about my strong point. Unfortunately, he had two arms.

I took note of my dangerous position. Even under normal conditions and with the strength of youth, a skier might be intimidated by the gorge that awaited a wrong decision. One had to be careful travelling this unpredictable edge, especially when one did not know where the edge was.

I caught myself. Why was I worrying about the edge at a time like this? The edge might be the solution. But no, the contract I had made with myself was that I must not be consciously reckless; I must not sit down on the job. I must keep going until I could go no more. If I went over the edge, that would be all right too, as long as it was honestly accidental, as long as I honestly tried to make it to the Gap. If I made it, I would be home free. For, although the Gap itself is an opening between two huge slabs of rock through which the wind slashes with the violence of knives, on the other side, because of the construction of the mountain, a wonderful peace and calm prevail. The ski-out, the Armageddon Run, is unbelievable. A variety of scoops and hills through metres of powder floats the skier safely home – if she is competent. If she is not, she should not attempt it, so say the books. The fact that I had been a good skier once should cover explanations to my family. They would think that once again I had miscalculated the situation. Or they might simply conclude that I had reached my dotage, for while sixty may not seem old to some, it is beyond ancient to one's twenty-something children.

If I did make it to my goal, I would push off and throw away my poles and my balaclava. I would close my eyes and hurtle myself into the unknown. I would end it in an insane wild leap into trees, rocks, oblivion. My last sensation on this earth would be the clean air rushing past my face, ice crystals forming on my eyes.

The idea of my body after death did not bother me much. Over winter, it would freeze solid. Then, whether it would rot and decay and be carrion for vultures or be stripped of flesh by the wind, in spring they would find my bones. But maybe not this spring. If I landed in some deep crevasse, the bottom of a creek, in a thick grove of trees, they might never find me. There must be hundreds, thousands, of unfound bodies – early explorers, settlers, skiers, climbers – in these mountains. The thought gave me comfort. I would not be alone. I was about to join a select club. Occasionally, someone found a heap of old bones – a heap just lying there in full view, a heap revealed by the melted snow, a heap once buried, uncovered by the wind. Then the forensic people got busy and tried to match those bones to their old reports of missing persons. Sometimes it all worked out, people found their long lost loved one. Other times, no one ever claimed the pile. Maybe those who once loved were also long gone. Maybe they did not read the news-paper. Maybe they had moved on.

I indulged myself a moment with the exciting thought of being found. It would be some time before the authorities confirmed car ownership and started looking. It would be some time before they found out I was not in Belize. A few months ago, a friend had been found dead in his apartment. He had been there for three months. Only two messages were on his telephone service. One was a wrong number and one was the local library telling him that if he didn't pick up his books, not only would they cancel his hold but charge him a fine. I mention him because he was the last straw in a long list of people I have betrayed through neglect, and if anyone had asked me, which they never did, I would say that was my fatal flaw, total unawareness of life.

Like my friend, I would lie in death quite a while before the system caught up with me, although unlike my friend I was not cut off from life, at least not physically. For starters, there was Aunt Olive who lived only two floors below me and Fred, her boyfriend. They were always wanting me to go with them to the dances at the Kerby Centre. Then there was Schmidt, the concierge – grey ringlets, thick glasses and ankles. For a while she would think that I had decided to stay longer on vacation. "That's funny," she'd think, cocking her head to one side the way she had a habit of doing. "Why didn't the old stringer tell me she'd be gone so long?" Not that she called me stringer to my face, but I had overheard her so describe me to another tenant.

Eventually, however, she would start to wonder at the burgeoning packet of mail beneath her counter. Not that I got much anymore, mostly bills and flyers and announcements of literary readings, even though I had not gone to one in years – the Writers Guild apparently never updates its list.

When my account ran out of maintenance payments – ah, yes, someone would inquire then. They did not let that go on too long in my building. But no one would think to look for me on a mountain. I had not skied in years except for the past month, when, to establish credibility, I had been out twice with an acquaintance. We had stayed on groomed trails, not like in the old days. I thought about the Alps, the Rockies, Colorado, the après-ski parties in the glittering lounges and restaurants, the soothing warmth of hot pools, the wonder of the snow falling softly on our naked shoulders.

Deep in my thoughts, I had laddered myself back several metres out of the wind, until the incline on my right sheltered me from the blast. This side of the bend was relatively calm.

Until now, in spite of the new snow, it had been business as usual, a matter of plodding up an incline of perhaps thirty degrees, mechanically poling, pushing one foot ahead of the other, keeping to the designated trail according to my mapping on the trail guide brochure in my pack. When they found me, I would look like a skier who had attempted too much; yet another casualty to these mountains.

I braced my poles in the snow and pushed up my goggles. Beneath my feet were ten metres of snow. Snow could shift, collapse, crack. I felt panic rising up in me. I pushed it down. I tried to think like my skiing husbands who never experienced such irrational thoughts and so could not understand a display of wobbly interior. This snow is not going anywhere until you're finished with it, I told myself sternly. I may have even spoken out loud. This snow was solid and sure. The avalanche hazard in this area was not high. One of the last things I had done before leaving my Eau Claire apartment the previous morning was to switch on the weather channel. Upon arrival at the Lodge, I had checked conditions with the nice young man at the desk. Snow, snow, and more snow, he had said, cheerfully. Good for business. Avalanche warning? Nah.

Yet, when I was getting out of my car, a loud shot shattered the crisp air and rang out across the stillness. Then, while strapping my boots into their harness, I heard the rumble of a distant train coming out of the mountain. Straightening, I had taken a long hard look at the scene before me, attempting to forage out of the blank white space its terrible secrets. The mountain had not so much as blinked in return.

Supporting myself with my poles, I removed one glove, shifted my pack, and reached inside for the 12K. I unsnapped the cap and put my glove back on. I needed that hand a little longer.

I looked back at the tracks I had made, two parallel lines in the snow, dark lines in the winter light, staining the pure unbroken expanse of white. I should have been pleased. Those lines meant I was almost to my goal. Instead, I was thrown into a state of intense agitation and distress. I had dared to mark the landscape. I had dared disturb this universe of silence with my pitiful mark upon it. I tried to explain to my rancher husband once, about being hypnotized by precise lines inscribed on white. I was just getting to the good part when out of the warm dark beside me in the bed came his rhythmic snore. Well, he did have to get up at four to start the spring branding.

I took a deep breath. The air was clean, full of the astringent odour of pine. Snow mounded the high crags and the sharp terrain beneath my feet. To my left, down an escarpment, lay the river valley some people would describe as breathtakingly beautiful, softly heaped with white, its spruce and pine bending with the grace of white. But I knew that the white was deceptive. It might look soft but it was hard. White bone, white skull. White is death in our cold climate. White can invade brain cells, occupy spaces of the mind. It can muffle you so that you can scream and scream but can't be heard. I hate white.

I used to like white. I used to like snow. I was strong, I was young, I was in love. And don't forget skilful. Skill is very important. All those years of skiing, it was such an adventure, such a challenge. In the white absence of an untried run, a presence, mysterious and ominous and exciting, lay waiting to be discovered like a story unfolding from nothing. But then white got into my head. I didn't tell my skiing husbands. They would not have understood. They saw white only as a surface on which to skim their boards.

I took small sips of the protein drink and thought how my hate included mountains. For if white is weight, mountains add to that weight. Why, then, had I chosen this place to die? In planning my venture, the scenario seemed so right, I could not choose another. A cruel place on the edge of a precipice, a place of discomfort. The place of challenge. The place of love. Love as hard white. Love as excavation of the soul, with jackhammer and drill bit, with knife and hatchet.

"Purple prose! Purple prose!" shouts Gully gleefully, having found me out in the mortal sin of heartfelt profundities. Was that the time I smashed the dinnerware?

A flurry of snow powder whipped around the bend. The trail around the bend was narrow. For an instant I hesitated. It was not too late to go back. I could lift myself up on my poles, do a one-eighty and ski back down in the tracks I had made. No one would ever know.

How like me to have trouble leaving the real world for the imagined one. Even though I was enacting my desire, even though I looked forward to the blessed relief of freedom from the soul-searching excavation process, I did not want to go around that bend.

I straightened my spine. I took a stance. I did not want the anguish of having to relive the events leading up to my decision, the unending replay in my brain, the intrusion of memory against my will. Like any sensible person, I tried to control my negative thoughts, but you can't choose what your brain relives. Life had become a downward spiral. The world was going to hell in a hand basket. Every morning the newspaper alerted us to another crisis. The city section was crammed with murders, home invasions, and people generally being downright nasty to each other. And on the home front, every time the phone rang it was Schmidt informing me of yet another permanent resident 'gone' and would I help on the memorial committee, a situation that, at my advancing age, I could only expect to continue.

As for my personal failures, I squirmed when I thought of them, which I suppose is why I didn't often do it. Suffice to say, I could not do relationships, as three marriages and four distant children should testify. And to top it all off, the creative impulse, with which I used to find some release, had deserted me. I was, indeed, in the valley of dry bones. My life had become the myth of Prometheus, the fellow chained to a rock and every day an eagle came along and ate his liver, which would grow back again at night so that the whole agony could be repeated the next day.

No one knew about my state. One does not go around with a bleeding liver hanging out. My waking hours were a frantic series of shopping trips, lunches, teas with friends desperate as myself to evade thoughts of broken relationships, lost children and grandchildren, in short, to evade life. Then, when I could escape no longer, hours that became eons of agony spent staring, simply staring. Night was a time of predictable torture, which I could not circumvent. I had not slept the sleep of careless age for several years. I was tired of the whole miserable mess. January 1st was the day I set to free myself from the rock.

January 1st, the first day of a brand new year, I had marked it on my calendar. January 1st, the day I used to start new writing projects. Beginning a manuscript in January, that saturnine time, may seem self-defeating. A better plan would be to attend endless parties, performances, lighted restaurants, gaudy bars. On the other hand, if you have the necessary fortitude to do so, it's a good month to jack up the thermostat, hunker down, hibernate and incubate.

Let's get the damned thing over with, I muttered beneath my stiff balaclava and heard Gully's snort of approval. Why the hell did I care what he thought? Why was I even thinking of him at a time like this? I jabbed the bottle to its place, swung my pack around to my back, tightened the strap and lifted my skis to a forward position. I remembered that the summit was not much further after the bend. I became inspired by the thought of the finish line, by the possibility of being successful at something, even if it was only contriving my own death. I bent my knees. I plunged my right foot forward, right, left, right, left, working the poles in coordination with the thrust of each ski. I tried to pace myself so I would not have to stop again. Right, left. Right, left. I concentrated on the tips of my skis as they ploughed a trail in a curve.

And then I was around the bend. And then I was struck with awe. The earth was a living moving thing, taking on new shapes by the instant. A fantastic ballet of various forms of white – the snow swirled into heaps, heaps that then took off with a life of their own, creating an evolving landscape that was both distorted and magical. I had forgotten that aspect of white. I had forgotten that it could be magic.

In this ever-changing terrain, I could not see where to place my skis. I could not see where terra firma was. Beneath my goggles, my eyes were tearing something fierce. I blinked hard twice. A sudden weakness in the bowels threatened to turn my insides out. Stay up, I told myself. Crawling is impossible.

Not only was my body failing, I was beginning to realize that my mind was no longer a reliable source of information. The trail suddenly seemed more difficult, the incline increasing, which should not be happening, according to the trail guide and my memory. Perhaps I was already suffering from hypothermia. I knew that a person can become deranged. I had seen occurrences of people raving incoherently because of constricting blood vessels and reduction of blood volume in the brain.

Within my cocoon of toque, hood, goggles, I could hear jagged, hoarse breathing, the whistle of air wheezing like bellows trying to fire up smoke-damaged lungs. God! Is that me? I wondered. It must be, I reasoned, there was no one else within miles. I was heaving now, like a broken animal, a dog we had on the ranch. She had been hit by a passing truck on the road. Her back legs were broken. She kept moving on her forelegs, dragging her hindquarters. I had to shoot her. I sent Lara back to the house for the gun. It breaks my heart, I said. You don't have a heart, Lara said. Ah, the bitterness in that young voice.

I snapped down a shutter in my brain. I had vowed not to think of my children, one still on the ranch with the man he thinks is his father, one away at school, one travelling to find himself; Lara, the only girl, lost to a cult in California.

A sharp pain flashed through my chest, the left side. The pain travelled down my left arm. For a moment I thought I was having a heart attack. With the nearest Emergency Station miles away down a hazardous mountain! Almost immediately, I realized how silly I was being. I had a heart like a horse. That was one of my problems. The old ticker could take any amount of battering and bruising, cracking and crushing, shattering and piercing, but it would not, simply would not, quit.

I could feel the chill of life. I could feel the warmth of death. I was quickly losing the heat of my body. If your heart and brain are cold, you cannot function normally. One more step, I chanted to myself. One more step.

If I made it to the summit, I might even sit and rest a moment before shoving off.

Trembling with weakness, wavering on my skies, buffeted by wind and whirling snow, I lifted my left foot. It seemed to take a long time. The ski felt like an immense weight. I tried to place my foot another stride upwards along the slope. The stride was more like a shuffle. I pushed my right foot and tried to place it alongside the other. The foot would not move on its own. I had to push it with my brain. Weakly, the right ski gabbled across the space and landed beside the other. The quivering knees had to straighten. After a long, doubtful struggle between my brain and my knees, my brain won. One more push. One more push. All movement was slow and painful. I could feel the cold in my core. I pulled my right ski pole out of the snow. The tip of the pole dislodged in slow motion. Flailing uncontrollably, I thrust up my arm with the pole in it and found a new spot in the snow. I forced my foot another step, I hauled up another foot of infinite weight. I lifted an arm and reached forward to place it in a new hold. I dragged a foot up to its new place.

I must go on fighting. I must go down fighting, with my boots on.

I have to sit down. I can't go any more.

I'm blanking out.

My mind prepared my body for the fall. I could have cried. Damn! Damn! Damn! Damn! I had been so close. My brain was reeling. My eyes were blinded by tears and cold. And my goddamn ski was lodged against something. The tip of my right ski had struck something. How can there be a tree root here? was my first thought, which, of course, was ridiculous. I squeezed my eyes tight to try to clear them. I saw in the winter sunless twilight a dark thing in the snow, a round shape that did not belong in that otherwise unmarked white.

I pushed my ski tip forward, prodding what at first I took to be an illusion. I shook my head. I looked again. I drew my ski back, attempting to disconnect it from whatever it had become entangled in. But it would not disconnect. It was stuck in the thing. I tore off my goggles, ripped off one glove, cleared my eyes with my bare hand. The most preposterous object assaulted my sight. My ski tip was stuck in the flesh of a human neck, in the soft flesh under the chin, except I could see right away that the neck and head were frozen stiff, the eyes frozen shut.

Again I blinked, several times. Hard. I slitted my eyes.

Shit, was my first thought. Fury was my first emotion. If that wasn't just like Harry, always interfering in my projects. Every goddamn time I got my life organized along came Harry with his crazy schemes. Jesus, Harry, I must have said it out loud through gritted teeth. For there, sticking up out of the snow was the head of, if not my first husband, certainly my first true love, a trickster if ever there was one.

2.

———⟨∞⟩———

*J*APANESE SKIER DIES AFTER FALL. *A forty-one-year-old Japanese woman was pronounced dead after falling from a cliff below Sadler's Peak. Members of the White Mountain Ski Patrol who responded to a report at 3:00 p.m. could not ascertain why the victim had been skiing in an out of bounds area. A rescue team rushed her to the ski base first aid station from where she was air-lifted to a Calgary hospital. The victim's name has not been released.*

That's not me, I thought. I'm not Japanese.

Third backcountry avalanche claims fifth victim this week.

My God! It was only Thursday.

And so far I had read only the front page of the newspaper. What other casualties might be lurking within? I opened the city section, snapped it straight, and read on.

I was in a large, bright room, windows on three sides, people in housecoats and slippers shuffling in and out, conversing in subdued tones. It certainly seemed real, as did the paper in my hand, but lately my take on reality was shaky. I had been drifting in and out of strange situations concerning dismembered heads and giant flying insects, which again, seemed real but apparently, were not. Or so the people in white coats said, assuring me that Harry's head was, in fact, attached to a body and that the whirring insect wings actually belonged to a helicopter. I thought about phoning Aunt Olive or Schmidt for confirmation of my existence but, quite frankly, did not

21

feel up to it. If either of them told me I was still in Belize then who was the person in this hospital bed? If I heard an out-of-body voice at the other end saying that the number I had dialed did not exist, I knew that I would break down into uncontrollable weeping.

Outside, the sun was shining, which was good because I was feeling pretty depressed at the idea of being alive. To think that that Japanese woman had achieved the death that I had planned! What's wrong with me? I screamed inside myself. I can't even kill myself successfully!

I could see through the window that it must be cold outside. Exhaust clouds escaped from cars, breath from people's mouths. On the walkway below, figures scurried along in parkas, toques, boots. A thick layer of snow covered what in summer must have been lawns and flowerbeds. I was sitting on a firm divan covered with cold vinyl material, something between mustard yellow and puce. Chairs of the same material were grouped about. A large table in the middle of the room contained a jigsaw puzzle, half completed. Several small tables were littered with books and papers. Not so long ago, they would have contained ashtrays, but now smoking was a criminal act.

I was dying for a cigarette.

Calgary climber swept to his death ... freak accident near Mount Livingston ... caught up in small avalanche ... unidentified man had planned a solo climb ... did not return as scheduled...

That could be Harry. I was not aware that he was living in Calgary, but there was no reason why I should be. He would not have phoned me with the news. Our encounters did not happen through a preconceived plan but, rather, when we got in each other's way.

RCMP and air rescue patrol launched a helicopter search...

I closed my eyes and saw again a giant insect with a whirring wing on top of its body hovering above a snow-covered incline. Long shadows like fingers crept across the bright morning snow.

Huddled into the snow, I stared at the shadows. They scurried around me like giant spindly legs. A darkness crept over me, a round, black shadow, the body of a giant spider with long legs. But it couldn't be a spider because it was flying in the sky. I couldn't look up to see what was causing the shadow or the sound because my neck seemed broken. But I could see its legs scurrying up the incline to one side of me.

I saw blinding white and against all that white, yellow, a yellow helicopter on skis, a man in its open door.

Even as I was being bundled onto the stretcher, I discerned men digging carefully into snow, digging around a head, the head I had spent the night with on the frozen white-bound cliff edge.

...body was discovered around nine a.m. ... pronounced dead at site ... identity has not been released pending notice of next of kin.

I felt a strange mixture of incredible relief and incredible sorrow. Harry would never bother me again. Never again would our paths cross. But he had been part of my life. A large part. If Harry was gone, something of me was gone – the Constance who had inhabited those delirious nights when we had flown like magical creatures. And, oh, those long conversations where we had sorted out the most profound thoughts, those phone calls from Gully, his "Did you hear, he's back in town." And off we would go, the three of us, holding hands, me in the middle, running to catch everything there was of life.

Who's going to make me smile now, I thought.

Spun off my foundation, suspended without direction in a vast cold inhuman space as formidable as the mountain, I had a moment of lost vision. Before my eyes, the black newsprint became hazy squiggles ... *intensive helicopter search ... body found in a crevasse...*

When I closed my eyes, I did not see a crevasse. I saw a snow-covered slope.

The black squiggles straightened themselves out and I read on.

How far the climber fell or what caused the fall has not been determined. Bad weather forced rescue team to suspend investigation.

I turned the page and read another headline: *Death trap trail...*

And another: *Avalanche hurls companion 200 metres down a 70-degree pitch ... bruised and battered ... survivor in hospital...*

Which is my story? I wondered. Which is Harry's? Who am I supposed to be?

I must have said the last out loud because a voice answered, "Constance DeForest."

I believed the authority of that voice – steady, devoid of inflection, containing certainty.

I lowered the newspaper. Across the top of it, filling one of the mustard/puce chairs, was a substantial grey presence – grey suit, grey overcoat, grey hat slanted at an angle around which I detected a rim of grey hair. The small blue eyes were absolutely steady and absolutely cold, as far as I could see. They were hidden beneath heavy eyebrows and the creases of a squint. The mouth was resolute, a tight straight line for lips. I did not doubt for an instant that here was a real man. He looked so *healthy*. Obviously, he was from the outside.

Against such a solid presence, I felt feeble, even tenuous. Against the smell of fresh cold on his coat, I was aware of the stale smell of my hospital dressing gown, of the faint aroma of antiseptic on my skin, of medication on my breath. I wished I had put on makeup, but this man would see through makeup.

He did not look like he would have a sense of humour, but he looked like he might know things. "You wouldn't happen to know...?" I hesitated.

The blue eyes did not flicker. The straight line remained tight.

"Which story is mine?" I gestured toward the paper in my lap. "There have been a lot of accidents lately in the mountains."

"There are always a lot of accidents in the mountains." His right hand reached beneath his overcoat. I felt alarm. It was the exact movement of the detective in film noir movies when reaching for a gun. But this man's hand continued beneath his suit jacket, into a breast shirt pocket. It came away empty. I recognized the movement of a man reaching for his cigarettes and felt some empathy for him.

He went on. "People think it's a playground. They don't realize it's a dangerous place." The hand that had reached for the cigarettes now took something from his overcoat pocket and flashed it before my eyes. "Sergeant Rock," he said, "Calgary City Police Department. I wonder if I might have a word with you."

What had I done wrong? Was suicide still a crime? I thought they had taken that off the books. Besides, how could he, anyone, know what I had attempted?

Diversion was called for. "How did they think to look for me? The search and rescue people."

"They weren't looking for you. It was the guy buried up to his neck in snow. He'd signed the register and hadn't returned." Sergeant Rock had such a disquieting way of looking at a person, his eyes so enshrouded you weren't sure where their scrutiny was being directed. "You didn't sign the park register."

Ahhh. That was why he was here.

"But wouldn't that be a federal offence? Since I was in a national park?" I wasn't trying to be smart. It was more a case of thinking out loud.

"That's not my business," he said. "I'm from the homicide division."

Homicide meant that someone was dead. My thoughts flew to Harry. But homicide also meant that somebody had killed somebody. Or tried to. "I thought it was an accident," I whispered.

"You thought what was an accident?"

Some instinct for self-preservation told me not to name names. "The head sticking out of the snow."

The sergeant must have caught a tremor of my skin, a twitch of my eye.

"Did you recognize that head?" he shot back.

I needed time to decide what I should admit to. "What happened?" I said. "I mean, out there on the mountain?"

"There was a localized avalanche in that area. He must have been swept down from the trail above."

"Ahhh," the light dawned.

"Yes?" A blue streak flashed briefly from between the fleshy creases.

I didn't think there would be any harm in telling him. "Just that I heard the crack. And the roar. From the parking lot. And then the trail around the bend, suddenly it got steeper. It wasn't supposed to do that."

"Just about killed him." The matter-of-fact voice interrupted my figuring.

"He's not dead!" My voice must have risen several notches, whether in relief or dismay, I was not sure, but the sergeant discerned a tone of familiarity.

"You know him then?"

"I'm surprised that anyone could survive a fall like that."

"He survived the fall, all right. He may even survive the hypothermia. Apparently, he was a large strong man. It's the jab to the jugular they're worried about."

"But how could I know!" I spluttered. "You can't possibly charge me with that! I didn't know I was jabbing anything, let alone a person!" I heard my voice rising to a shrill.

"Don't excite yourself. You've been through an ordeal." The straight lips flicked up and down like the snap of a whip, a fleeting smile perhaps meant to reassure me. It didn't. "We know he had an accident. In fact, likely you saved his life by erecting the emergency shelter you had in your pack."

"I did? Erect it, I mean?"

"You don't remember?"

"No. But I must have. I mean, if one was erected. I was the only one there. It must have been instinct." Ah, life, I thought. What a strange beast. My children who so resented Harry, had saved his life, for I would not have carried a full survival pack if not for the appearance of things for their sake.

With his right hand Sergeant Rock took a notebook and the stub of a pencil out of his pocket. His manner clearly stated that the chitchat was done and it was time to get down to business. I realized that hysterics would get me no place with this man. I must keep calm, keep my wits about me. "I was trying to get to the summit and the ski-out when all of a sudden my ski tip hit something in the snow," I said, as if by rote, keeping my voice in a monotone. "It was quite a shock when I realized that it was the head of a man."

"You weren't companions?"

"No."

"You're sure?" Again, those blue squinty eyes.

"Of course I'm sure."

"Somebody was."

That wasn't surprising. Harry always had a companion.

"Somebody signed the register with him, but we can't make out the name. We're not even sure whether it's male or female."

It would be female, I thought but kept my mouth shut.

"No one has come forth. No one has made inquiries. That could mean that somebody's missing. Out on that mountain. The RCMP will be contacting you in hopes you can help them."

"I don't know anything. I don't know who his companion might have been. I don't know him." Sadly, I realized the truth of my statement, although once we had been the closest of companions. "I just happened upon him," I said clearly, then much to my consternation started to babble. "From what I've been reading in the paper, those mountains are like rush hour on the freeway. No wonder people run into one another." I could hear my voice rising again. I became aware of other patients in the room looking in our direction. I clamped my lips.

Sergeant Rock flipped open the notepad, produced the palmed pencil and began to write, all with the same hand. Interview – Constance DeForest, Jan. 4th – I read the letters upside-down.

They meant that I'd escaped Constance DeForest for three days. What a blessed three days it must have been. Too bad, I couldn't remember most of it.

His hand stopped writing. He looked up. "Your car was missing registration documents." It was an accusatory statement.

"Really?" I feigned surprise. "Do you suppose someone came along and stole them?"

He gave me the eye. "We checked out the license plate." He looked down. "We spoke to someone named..." He flipped his pad back a page, "...Schmidt this morning." He looked at me with disapproval. "You're supposed to be in Belize."

"Oh that," I said feebly. "I changed my mind."

"You didn't tell anybody."

"Surely, that's not a crime."

"No. But when there's been a murder, you look for things that don't fit." While balancing the notepad on his knee, he again put his hand into his pocket. This time he brought out a photo. He held it toward me. He did not look at the photo. He looked at my face looking at the photo. "Do you know this man?" he asked.

I tried to keep the shock of recognition from flashing across my face. "No." It wasn't really a lie. The man in the photograph was a totally different person than the husband of my salad days when I believed everything I was told.

I thought I had kept my voice steady, but he insisted. "Take a closer look." His hand was firm on the photograph. I kept my hands in my lap. Then I realized that I was not being co-operative, which might go against me. I took the photo.

There was the sonuvabitch's face all right – grey wispy hair, moustaches twirled, phony smile. He was wearing a deer-hide shirt. I had seen the photo before. It was the same one that had been in a newspaper article. For, while I had not seen him in the flesh for a long time, over the years, I had seen his mug everywhere. I couldn't avoid it. No one could, not if they watched television or read newspapers. He was a regular on talk shows, radio interview slots, the arts and entertainment sections. He kept winning awards, topping the bestseller lists, getting married and divorced, getting into fights, insulting reviewers. And then there were the literary magazines and dust jacket covers.

I shook my head. In fact, I knew that face as well as I knew my own.

"Are you sure?"

"Yes," I said. What's he done now? I thought.

"That's funny," he said. "Seeing as how you were married to him."

I looked up quickly. The facial expression was not mocking, not threatening, not even interested. Sergeant Rock was a relaxed man, his manner casual. But his body gave the impression of a powerful contained energy, as though at any moment it could be ready to leap at its prey.

Of course the police would have my information. It would be on record. Our marriage had not been a secret. Why had I foolishly lied? Because I did not want to be mixed up in any of Gully Jillson's shenanigans. I pretended to look at the picture again. "You can't blame me for making a mistake, " I said. "He looked nothing like this when we were married. That was," I thought a moment, "thirty years ago."

"Thirty-five, according to the date on the marriage certificate." He took back the photo.

"Thirty," I countered, "according to the date on the divorce certificate."

He chose to ignore my contention, as if it was not worth debating. "When was the last time you saw him?"

I decided to tell the truth as long as it didn't incriminate me. "I can't remember exactly. It's been a long time. And that was just a passing nod at a literary function."

It finally struck me that this policeman was asking a lot of questions without telling me why. Wasn't that unconstitutional or something? I tried to recall TV police shows. "Don't you have to read me my rights?" I said. "At least tell me what this is all about." I nodded toward the photo. "What does he have to do with the accident?"

"Nothing," said Sergeant Rock. "At least the accident in the mountains. That's not why I'm here. We're investigating a possible homicide."

So, somebody had finally murdered the SOB. I was only mildly surprised.

"We'd like to get in touch with this man and ask him some questions."

Not him, then. But even though Gully and I had not parted on the most amicable terms, I could not let them think what the sergeant was thinking. Confidence man, yes. Murderer, no. "Gully wouldn't be involved in something like that," I said.

"He was seen at the scene of the crime. The evening of January 1st."

My brain was stunned. To think that was the very night I was dying out on that mountain.

"By Mrs. Schmidt." That blue scrutiny wouldn't let me off the hook.

"But that's my building. How very odd."

"That's what we think, too."

"Who is the victim?" I held my breath.

"A woman who might have been mistaken for you. She lived in the apartment directly below you. We're exploring the possibility that you might have been the intended victim. Because of your husband ... former husband"

"That's impossible!" My brain tried to light on what he had just said. "He'd know it wasn't me he was murdering."

"Not necessarily. Not if it was dark."

What the sergeant suspected was total nonsense. I was the one who should want to murder Gully, not the other way around. Unless it was to cover up his source material. But was that worth murder? Maybe to Gully it was.

"What was her name?"

"I'll ask the questions if you don't mind." His gaze was steady on my face, which must have shown consternation. "How well did you know this woman who lived below you?"

"Not at all." My lips were numb. "I didn't know her at all. I know nothing about her. Schmidt might know."

"We have a statement from Schmidt. I'm now obtaining a statement from you."

He wrote in his notebook. "Did you ever see her?"

"No. Once maybe. On the elevator. It might have been her. A couple of months ago, a woman got into the elevator on the eleventh floor. I hadn't seen her before. There'd been some gossip among the permanent residents about the sexy new neighbour." I didn't elaborate on this point because it contained Aunt Olive's reaction to Fred's reaction to the new tenant. "She stepped in like she owned the place and pushed the down button the same way. I remember because I thought I recognized her but couldn't recall from where or when. She reached across me, pushed the 'close' button, and said, impatiently I thought, "*If* you don't mind.""

"Can you describe her? Tall? Short? Skinny? Fat?"

"A trashy Jackie Collins type."

"What does that mean?"

I looked at the sergeant. He wouldn't be into Jackie Collins heroines. I doubt he read anything but police reports. "Big hair, big lips, big makeup, big boo…, high heels, expensive stockings, great legs." The total opposite of me, I thought but kept it to myself. Something occurred to me. "Why are you asking me to describe her? Don't you know? From the body?"

"As a matter of fact, we don't. Anonymous phone call. All the elements of a crime scene, blood, weapon, signs of violence, but no body. Still, we have to investigate. Did you ever see anyone with her?"

"No."

Sergeant Rock looked down at his notes. He looked up. "Did your former husband know your place of residence?"

I felt a strange urge to defend Gully Jillson, in spite of the fact that he was an asshole. "No. And the fact that he was seen leaving the building on the same night a murder happened there doesn't mean anything. He could have been dining in the restaurant. It's quite a popular one."

"He was spotted entering the elevator." The sergeant flipped his notepad back a few pages. "At ten p.m. on the evening of January 1st, Mrs. Schmidt from her place at the desk saw a strange man enter the building and then enter the elevator. Knowing he was not a registered guest and suspicious of him being a guest of a resident because of his unkempt appearance and furtive manner, she followed him onto the elevator. There, her suspicions were confirmed as he pushed the button for the twelfth floor. She was sure no one on that floor," Rock looked up and down, "would have him for a visitor. Mrs Schmidt, not wanting to appear obvious, stayed on the elevator and went back down to the eleventh floor with the intention of taking the stairs up a flight. There, she was surprised to see again the intruder entering the corridor via the stairwell door. He had a furtive air." Rock held the page at some distance. "Furtive." He brought it back closer to his face. "Sneaking around, like."

Rock looked at me straight on. "Since nine out of ten homicides are committed by the spouse or boyfriend, in the case of females, that is, we showed Schmidt your former husband's photo which we got off the Internet. Her reaction, and I quote...," he looked down at his notes, "he looks too clean." He looked up. "Upon further questioning, she was able to make a positive identification that it was the same man."

Sergeant Rock put the photo back into his pocket. In doing so, he leaned closer to me, so close I could smell the tobacco on his suit jacket. It smelled heavenly.

"I wonder if you could tell me in some detail," he said, "the exact circumstances of the last time you saw your former husband?"

I did not answer. I could not. For in that moment, when he leaned forward, I saw that the lower left sleeve of his jacket was empty, that the hem of it was folded neatly into his jacket pocket. My heart began to beat very fast. It was out before I thought. "Were you once a ranch hand in the Porcupine Hills?"

3.

———⊶⊷———

T HE NIGHT OF THE DAY of Sergeant Rock's visit to the hospital, I made the long journey down the hall to the intensive
care unit, not easy because I was not in the best shape myself.
My internal temperature, in conjunction with Harry's, seemed
to have lowered several degrees. The head on the flat hospital
pillow, spotlighted by the night-light above, was large. With
its broad bony forehead, pronounced cheekbones, deep eye
sockets, it looked like the skull of a bull with a mane of wispy
white hair. I detected the faint odour of formaldehyde.

The body was flat on its back beneath a mound of blankets,
one electric, the cord hanging down the side of the mattress
and running to a wall socket. The blankets were tucked up
close under his chin, his hands and arms hidden. They must
have been trying to thaw him out. When I had inquired about
him earlier, the nurse on duty at the desk told me that he was
comatose.

I wondered if he was faking it. For, if Gully had missed his
calling as a con artist, Harry had missed his as an escape artist.
He might have been the Great Houdini himself. More than once,
I had witnessed his disappearing act with women, quicksilver
between shafts of light, the Venetian blinds swinging to rest,
and he was gone in the early morning, leaving behind the faint
odour of his sweat on the sheets, some teary ingénue for me
to console, and a draft of poems I had managed to squeeze
out during his visit.

He can't escape now, I thought. He's too old and sick. Why did I feel sad?

Those crazy days, those white nights, the pursuit of the ineffable, the spirit of that pursuit which we had shared, another case of life becoming past fiction.

In spite of the fact that he had tubing in his nostrils, tubing that was hooked up to an oxygen tank, he seemed to be having trouble breathing, as if he couldn't draw air deep into his lungs. Perhaps his lungs, too, were still frozen, perhaps they had been permanently damaged. Another length of tubing led from a suspended bottle down and beneath his blanket. I looked at the deep creases in the bloodless skin, at the bush of hair. Be very, very, careful, I told myself. This is the man who deserted you ten years ago. Took off, just like that, without a word. When you phoned all you got was the message, "this number has been discontinued." But you survived. You got your life together. Don't start back where you left off.

His face was fixed in an expression of bland disinterest. I must have stared for ten minutes but not a muscle of his features moved. I felt myself becoming angry.

"You were stalking me," I hissed, remembering that it was the middle of the night in a public hospital. "Don't deny it. Every time I've got my life sorted out and forgotten all about you after months of crying into my pillow, then, by god, if you don't turn up again. I'm sick and tired of it. Every time I get a breakaway for life, there you are, tripping me up. I won't have it, I tell you."

I imagined he groaned and tried to say something like, stop, please, go away.

"I have no intention of going," I said, "until I've had my say. I want you to leave me alone. Do you hear?"

I thought his mouth twitched but I may have been hallucinating again, a condition I was prone to since the mountain caper. I looked more closely. His expression had turned to one of pain. I supposed that meant he was still alive. But I knew that you couldn't trust his pain. Pain for him was a source of enjoyment. He embraced it with masochistic gusto.

"What were you doing there?" I went on. "How could you have the *audacity* to ruin my plans? You always ruin my plans. You ruined my life."

I hadn't realized that I had raised my voice. Next thing I knew, a white-capped nurse came bustling in, flapping like a barnyard hen with the rooster loose. "What are you doing?" Her whisper was frantic. "Who are you? Visitors are not allowed in the intensive care unit." And more of the same.

Frankly, I was surprised. My experience in hospitals was that you could be gasping your last breath and no one would pay the slightest attention. However, it was a good thing she came along. I was so furious at that frozen face, that frozen silence, I might have yanked that IV right out of that frozen arm.

Instead, I took him home. What else could I do?

"We know you're in there."

In the melancholy light of winter, I stood looking down at the head on my pillow and listening to the tired monotone of Sergeant Rock, a voice that pursued me even into the recesses of my most private space. Why was I surprised? When he interviewed me in the hospital, even then I had pegged him as a man who would not give up until he had pinned down the adversary. A week had passed since I had blurted out that sappy remark about the ranch hand and I still grew hot with shame at the memory. Rock did not look the least bit like my old love, a tall, lean man reminiscent of a young Clint Eastwood. It was just that I had been so thrown for a loop by the absence of that arm.

"May I remind you, Ms. DeForest, that we are conducting a homicide investigation." The answering machine was downright snappy.

It was my own fault. I could have buried the phone in the deep freeze, or put it in the kitchen with the sound turned down, but it might have been one of my children wanting money. It might have been the hospital checking on Harry. If I didn't answer those calls, they would take him back. They had only let me have him because of a bed shortage crisis that was rampant in our city hospitals.

It might have been Aunt Olive needing me, although at the moment I was avoiding discussions with my dear aunt because she was off on a tangent. "What's with this *Ser*-geant Rock?" She was on the phone the minute he got out the door after interviewing her.

"What do you mean?" I pretended ignorance.

"You know what I mean. He has only one arm."

"Why doesn't he take off his hat?" I ignored her implication. "The last guy I knew who never took off his hat, when he finally did, he was totally bald underneath."

"A man can do worse things than be bald," she said.

As for the murder, I did not need Sergeant Rock to tell me the news. Aunt Olive and Schmidt more than kept me informed on that subject. As could be expected, the entire building was a buzz of excitement. We had not had a murder before. As soon as I arrived home from the hospital, The Permanent Resident Committee informed me that it was organizing a memorial to be held in the common room, collecting for flowers and a soloist. Apparently, some tense moments were encountered at the planning meeting when members of the refreshment committee took sides as to whether the lunch would be cold sandwiches or hot casseroles but, as Schmidt opined when telling me all about it, it would not be fitting to have cold sandwiches in winter. Naturally, we would not be honoured by the appearance of the *corpus delicti*. Even the police so far had not been so honoured. One member of the committee brought up that very subject. "What if she isn't dead?" But the others shouted her down. The majority wanted a mid-winter party in spite of the fact that no one had known the guest of honour. She had been a permanent resident for only three months. The majority ruled that since no friends or relatives had come forth, it was up to us in the building to do the Christian thing. "Such a lovely woman, too." Schmidt, who as far as I knew had not spoken more than two words to her, heaved a great sigh at the other end of the line. "Ah well, it just goes to show, life's a mystery. You never know what's in store for you."

Why Rock wanted to talk to me was another mystery. He had interviewed me extensively in the hospital and I could supply no further clues. True, I had not told him about the blood on my carpet. When I arrived home from the hospital there it was, a rust-coloured smear on the white carpet inside my door. To put it mildly, I was upset. I was so proud of that carpet. I could never have had a carpet like that on the ranch, with the kids tracking in mud from the corral and hay from the barn and the cats carrying in dead birds and mice and the dogs dragging in manure on their feet and on their swishing tails.

In my defence, I was not even sure it was blood. Lots of other things look like blood. If it had not been for the murder in the building, I would have assumed it was from a wet leaf or the red shale on the river walk where I exercised regularly. When did I do that? I wondered when down on my hands and knees rubbing the spot with carpet stain removal. I was always careful to remove my footwear on the square of protective plastic in front of the door. Only later did it occur to me that it *might* be blood. My first thought was, what are the charges for removing evidence vital to a murder investigation? I don't want an anthill of police and forensic types crawling over the apartment finding out about Harry, was my second thought.

I supposed I would have to answer Rock sooner or later. But I could not bear to interrupt my time with Harry. And Harry was not Rock's department. On that score, the Missing Persons police had informed me that they wanted to talk with Harry as soon as he came to. Apparently his companion on the mountain had not turned up.

"If you refuse to cooperate, you leave us with no alternative but to obtain a court order..." The relentless invisible voice continued.

Meanwhile, the voice I wanted to hear eluded me.

After two weeks of me pacing my room from bed to bathroom to bed to window to bed, the heavenly kingsize that I had given up for Harry, of standing over him for hours alongside his IV pole, of sitting in a chair beside him, staring, watching for the twitch of a muscle, I was still left wondering if that head was going to light up, if it was going to speak to me, reveal its contents, reveal to me its dreams of winter, dreams of landscape.

I thought how the bed resembled the mountain – smooth and white with a ridge along one edge, which was Harry. Blankets were pulled up around his head, close and tucked in around the ears, just like the hospital ordered. His eyes were closed, the sockets two sunken holes overhung by the dense shrubbery of his eyebrows. His lips, which I remembered as being expressive, even sensual, were now thin and tight, like a prisoner's refusing to give information. His skin had lost its under layer of flesh to the snow and the elements, lost it to the landscape of his dreams and was greyer than his grey beard, grey in contrast to the white pillowcase. He was old and tired, his face emaciated with suffering. But he couldn't be suffering now, I decided. People in comas didn't suffer, did they?

Nearly two weeks had passed since he had been buried in the snow and still he was frozen to the marrow of his bones, figuratively speaking. The hospital gave me a list of instructions. Keep warm. Try warm fluids. His vitals signs were on the chart, squiggles on the low end. Eventually, according to the people in the know, he would thaw out, or not. They cited cases of people who had been in comas for twenty years.

I left him only long enough to prepare chicken broth. In addition to the intravenous kit supplied by the hospital, I was to spoon this broth into him. A slow procedure it was, the liquid dribbling back out the corners of his mouth, but the doctors wanted me to keep trying. I had to make sure it wasn't too hot or too cold. The cold seemed to congeal in his throat, but I didn't want to burn those valuable vocal cords either; they were all I had left to remind me of my grandfather. I was concerned about nourishment, but the hospital people assured me that when the metabolism is almost non-existent, the requirement for food is small.

I had pulled an old fold-up cot out of the closet, one I kept on hand in case my children should all happen to visit at once, which wasn't likely since they scarcely ever visited even singly, but hope does not die easily in the human specimen. I had placed the cot near Harry's side of the bed, within arm's reach, in case he needed anything in the night, but he never did. Once I tried to have a shower. I was on the edge of the stall, one foot raised to step across the rim, when, through the jetting water, I thought I heard a cry from the other room. I jumped out immediately, threw a towel around me, ran to the bed and stood there staring until my eyes watered. I didn't dare blink in case I missed some movement, some twitch of muscle.

I should have felt triumphant – Harry's head delivered to me on a snow platter, Harry's body in my bed. Was that not what I once had longed for? But like so much in life, it had happened too late and out of context. I hadn't wanted it for some years now. Our last confrontation had been shortly after my last marriage. I bumped into him in a crowded airport. He seemed preoccupied, looking for his current companion in the crowd at the departure gate. I turned the other way and followed my husband to a life of travel and distraction.

Not only did I not care any more, I found the agitation his presence always caused in me to be uncomfortably upsetting. When I was young, I had exulted in the excitement of him. When I was close to him, I was alive. Now I did not want to be alive, I was too tired. I was finished with all that fly-me-to-the-moon foolishness. What I felt now was irritation. He had gotten in the way of my plan. He had brought me back to life and for what?

It was a puzzle that was causing me a great deal of anxiety, even fear, for I knew I would have to solve it and I was not sure that I could. And now I could not die before working it out, before knowing what I was supposed to do with Harry.

I knew the danger. In order to keep him alive, we might have to form a deep bond. I broke out into a cold sweat. Deep bonds were not my thing. To have to go forward and do something when you have failed at that thing, not once but many times, was the sort of dilemma that could cause neurosis, maybe even psychosis, at the very least upset stomach and bad breath. As I stood looking down at that head that showed not a flicker of animation, something in me warned that it was too late. The situation was pure fantasy. Something else said I had to try, that destiny was calling. For why else would Harry appear in my path when I was struggling toward my death? Why, by some quirk of fate, when I was trying to die had I, with my flimsy emergency tent, been given this person to keep alive? Not any person, but the very person who had caused me to run off and leave supper in the fridge for my children, who had induced me to neglect family and friends, who had inspired me to betray a perfectly good husband by bringing home a one-armed out-of-work ranch hand he had met in the local bar, and finally, who had deserted me?

I turned away toward the window and stared at the snow and tried to breathe in a regular pattern.

Since my apartment was on the twelfth floor and faced out to blank space, I had not bothered with drapes. At each side of the window hung vertical Venetian blinds that could be pulled against the sun if necessary. My view faced north and the Bow River, a pleasant aspect, especially in summer when the trees were leafy and full. Now, I could see nothing outside the window except snow.

I thought of the problem of beginnings, specifically the beginning of a different relationship between Harry and me. Never before had we co-habited. Indeed, we had always been co-habiting with other people. Chance meetings, occasional flings, avid discussions at seminars and in bars after seminars, always in a group of like-minded individuals; that had been our relationship. Magically, he would appear in town. After a few crazy nights, off he would go again. Even in those ranch years, when we settled down to being friends, he arrived as a visitor inhabiting the guest room, usually with a female companion.

To live with a person, to achieve a regular routine of domesticity, was a totally different matter. Could we do it? For me, it became a question of what I should do with him. Sex was out of the question, at least until he was thawed out. Of course, I am being facetious. While our relationship had embodied physical attraction and a lot of flirting, it had never been consummated. Such gross, if not comical, behaviour might have spoiled things and I, for one, had not wanted to take that chance. Our deeper connection had been, dare I say, spiritual, something in us calling to each other. Perhaps it was the landscape we shared, for we were both born on the prairie, both born to loneliness and desolation.

When was our beginning? I tried to think. When is the beginning for any two people? When they first see each other, when they are introduced, when they touch, when their minds first connect?

Against the snow pattern on the glass, I saw him standing beside a long oak bar on a cold winter night, reading to about thirty people. I was an undergraduate student at the university, working toward a degree in Education, with a major in English. A fellow student who had the hots for her professor, who was scheduled to read, had dragged me along to the event. The professor was already a writer of some renown and, in spite of the fact that he had a partner, attracted a gaggle of females constantly at his heels. He had a reputation for having insatiable appetites and incredible technique, perhaps because of the steamy and raucous sex scenes in his novels. Personally, I was not impressed or intrigued. I have always thought that explicit and steamy sex in novels means that the writer is either impotent or incompetent in that regard.

My companion and I shuffled into a dimly lit bar where a scattering of students and Calgary literati huddled in out of the cold. Rustling and removal of coats, murmuring and petty gossip, the ordering up of beers, these are the sounds I remember. And all these years later, I can still smell the damp cold of overcoats freshly removed and hung on chair backs and feel the discomfort of those wooden chairs.

Being a serious student with no funds backing me except those from a small scholarship and my part time job at Earl's, being older because I had worked for some years after high school to save money, I was always on the periphery. Because of my job and wanting to keep up my grades for future scholarships, I did not have time to properly do the student thing. My companion was a very pretty curvaceous classmate whose parents had money and who had latched onto me the first day of class. I think she saw me as a pitiful specimen totally unfit to survive on my own. In this she was right. I remember an end of class party in someone's basement where I accepted what I thought was a regular cigarette, an action that had disastrous results, the details of which are unnecessary to go into here. The literary reading, if I remember correctly, was to be part of my education. My friend ordered us both glasses of Donini and I thought how I should be home preparing for exams.

Approximately half an hour after the appointed start, my anxiety over my exam escalating by the minute, a thin man with a scraggly beard ambled up to the front. Slowly, the murmurings and bustle subsided. He said a few words of blessing, thanked everybody who was remotely connected to the endeavour, made a few announcements about future literary events, then introduced the featured reader, who was sitting near the front and jumped to his feet, lightly for a man so large. My companion nudged me. I tried to show an interest. He did have a certain flair, certainly a presence, and he was quite attractive for an older man approaching forty.

Then he opened his mouth. He spoke. Harry – for of course the professor my friend had the hots for was Harry – spoke. It was the voice of my grandfather! My grandfather, my first erotic experience. Oh, nothing kinky. All aboveboard. I sat on his lap and he hugged me and kissed me and told me stories in a wonderful deep, husky, soft, whisky-cured, cigarette-smoked raspy voice. Suffice to say, when I heard that same voice, the voice of my heritage, my place in the world – the long light of a northern forest, the cool green bell-ringing pastures of summer evenings, the long white silence of winter – I was powerless before the force that swept over me.

After that, someone read a poem about laughing lilacs. Another person read a poem from the point of view of grass, the kind you cut with a lawnmower. A third person mumbled an incoherent jumble of words, whether poetry or prose I could not tell.

Next thing I knew, my friend ran up to the front to gush and exclaim. I turned and ran as fast as I could out of the bar, out onto the snowy winter street. When I calmed down, I found myself on a city transit bus going in the wrong direction.

I did not pursue him. He was in a relationship. He was old. He was a teacher, the voice of authority, a high priest of learning, a cloistered monk. It was only later I realized the real reason – he raised in me something that was too large. I could not face the emotions he threatened me with.

Urged by my friend, I signed up for his course in Canadian literature. Imagine him naked, she whispered across the aisle to me during a lecture. I was shocked. The physical was not my purpose. However, even though I made myself as unobtrusive as possible, the chemistry between us was palpable. When passing by his desk, I felt vibrations. I was sure he felt the same vibrations. I caught him looking at me from time to time in class, as if begging for an answer, which I was always too shy to render. When we met in the hall, he seemed pleased to see me, although in all honesty I have to say that, being a congenial man, he seemed pleased to see most people. But I knew, I just knew, that he was attracted to me. However, he always had a partner. Shortly thereafter, I always had a husband. But that wasn't the point. We might have been friends then, rather than later, but I was too much of a coward even for that. Even our friendship would have demanded the burden of more commitment than I could manage.

Instead, I started writing poetry, abysmal poetry, nonetheless poetry. All the long winter, watching his mouth open and close, listening to the voice of my grandfather, scarcely noting what it was saying, I sat in the back and wrote furiously in my notebook. Thus, in total ignorance of what poetry should be, I produced my first volume, poems about frozen sloughs, tree skeletons and sullen winter skies, inspired by stories my grandfather told me about endurance on a northern Alberta homestead. I called the volume simply *Winter*. A small press took pity on me and printed one hundred copies, seventy of which to this day remain in storage in the bowels of my building.

At the end of the semester, the class went to Dinny's Den for a windup. I was thwarted in my attempt to sit next to the teacher but at the end of the evening he sought me out and gave me a big hug. That night in my bed, I felt the strength of his arms around my body, the rough tweed of his jacket on my cheek. The comfort of his bear chest soothed my senses and lulled me to sleep. I wasn't dense enough not to see that he hugged a lot of people that night, in fact, just about everybody, but I knew that there was a special meaning in the hug he gave me.

Then Harry left, without so much as a good-bye. I heard he had moved to another part of the country. I did not expect to see him again. But after that, every time I got my life together, every time I married and bought some furniture and settled down to normalcy, every time I had a child and decided to do some serious nurturing, Harry would raise his head. In a newspaper column, I would learn that he was in town for a performance. In the *Alumni Magazine* I would read that he was giving a series of lectures. Through the grape vine, I would hear that he was conducting a workshop. And off I would traipse, leaving my current partner to look after the baby.

Thus, I lived my life, raising a family, keeping a house, having dinner parties, banging out articles for magazines and publishing now and then a slim volume of poetry which the critics felt lacked power.

When I ran into him on the mountain, I had left my lyrical voice far behind. I can honestly say that Harry had become a dim memory of youth and poetry. My last volume, *North* – poems about shelling peas, cleaning wool, and burning potato beetles, all against a barren background of echoing barns and desolate farm houses – had been critically ignored. My last husband turned out to have gobs of money so I could pay the rent. Until I descended into the funk that propelled me to the mountain, for something to keep me occupied, I had worked at my small career. Writing freelance articles demanded little of me apart from research time and putting sentences together in an orderly fashion. I especially liked documenting prairie history, perhaps because it pleased Aunt Olive, my grandfather's child. In short, I was content most days. As for happiness, I viewed it a fancy of youth and ignorance. I did not want Harry back in my life. I did not welcome the discomfort of a fibrillating heart. When, occasionally, I thought of him, it was with a smirk at the memory of an otherwise serious student in her mid-twenties acting like a silly schoolgirl, a romantic fool who had called him from a pay phone in the middle of the night and, when he answered, held her breath until he hung up, who, for the rest of her life waited for a return phone call that never came. My rational self knew that it was totally unreasonable to expect Harry would phone me. Even if he had recognized my silence, why should he call? What would he have said? But my heart told me that he *should*. He was not doing his part in the pursuit of our common destiny.

When I ran into Harry on the mountain, I had long given up all that romantic drivel about destiny, common or otherwise. But standing in that shadowy room, staring at the relentless snow, I came to the conclusion that Harry had been put in my path for a reason and, even if he was refusing to do his part, it was time for me to do more than mine. How something begins is how it unfolds, so goes the old saying. If our destiny was going to be fulfilled, I would have to change. I would have to stop running in the opposite direction, stop viewing him from a safe distance, stop hiding in a group, stop hiding in the married state.

I turned back to the room. On both sides of the bed were night tables. One was bare except for a lamp. The other was piled with books and pills and a clock alarm. As a rule, I spent a lot of time there not sleeping. What I did in bed was read and make notes for articles and, to that end, I had furnished the room with broadloom on the floor to muffle sound and only a few good undemanding prints on the walls. I had mounded the bed with white woolly cozy blankets.

As I stood over Harry pondering the inconceivable, I heard again the voice of doom, "You may be next. You may be fingered for death."

Sergeant Rock was right, although not in the way he meant. The fact was, the years were piling up at an alarming rate. Time was not on my side. Suddenly, my legs ached with fatigue. I felt like a sick child. I wanted my comfy quilt, my bunny and my homo milk. Something propelled me around the end of the bed and ordered me to stretch out on top of the blankets, straight on my back, hands folded across my chest, in much the same position as Harry.

At first I could not breathe. I had never before been on a bed with Harry in the flesh. The sensations at being so close to my heart's desire stopped me completely. My innards were trembling like a volcano on the verge of explosion. My nerves were like elastic bands twanging all over the place, threatening to snap. I forced myself to take deep breaths. I turned my head.

The long mound of Harry beneath the white blankets was like the low hill beside our farmhouse where we used to sled in winter. The possibility of the voice of my grandfather was as close to me as Harry beside me on this bed. That was when it came to me. I knew what I had to do, what fate was compelling me to do. I would finally write that quintessential prairie novel I had long promised Aunt Olive.

4.

⸙

I WAS READING AN ARTICLE in the *Globe and Mail* about literary lushes and considering becoming one when a knock came at the door. It wasn't really a knock. It wasn't a knock at all. It was the buzzer on my intercom. I heard a knock because I was thinking about Poe's Raven. Once upon a midnight dreary and so on. Suddenly I heard a knocking, quoth the Raven evermore. According to the article, Poe was one such lush.

I was drinking coffee and going through the piled-up newspapers. Winter was still raging outside the glass. It seemed we were in the middle of yet another blizzard. I'd had that shower I'd kept promising myself. I'd washed my hair, brushed my teeth. I had slathered a sweet smelling lotion all over my body and put on my fuzzy robe. I had even creamed my face and put on a little eye shadow and lipstick. I was feeling mighty fine and all because the Head, as I'd come to think of Harry, had winked at me. Jesus, women are pitiful creatures, I thought. One wink from that huge bearded head and I'm in ecstasy. How needy, how hopeful, how pathetic.

I had no intention of taking a long break. For what might follow that wink? Still, I thought a break would energize me for what lay ahead, so I'd made a very large pot of coffee and had settled down on the sofa to get snapped on caffeine, nicotine and the *Globe and Mail*. I was reading the part about Poe's death being an enactment of the final days of Roderick Usher, thinking how life copies art, a phenomenon which I have found uncanny in my own life, when, as I say, the buzzer sounded. I decided to ignore it.

Some critics and researchers try to see writers as a community linked by shared sensibilities, by a common interest in the great vowel shift or by an exquisite sensitivity to the role of sibilance in poems about snakes. The truth is more prosaic: writers, in the main, are drunks and always have been.

I lifted my head and stared at the snow pattern on the huge picture window. I took a drag of my cigarette and stroked my chin, noting absent-mindedly, the long hair like my grandmother's I had failed to tweeze. Jesus, I thought. If that's all it takes. I can do that. I lowered my head and started reading again.

Life as a long sickness. The white logic that speaks to danger and certain doom.

The buzzer sounded again.

Again, I ignored it. Likely, someone collecting for homeless gerbils. Everyone in my usual circle of lunch and shopping dates thought I was still in Belize. Only Schmidt and Aunt Olive and the permanent residents knew I was here, although Schmidt's manner toward me indicated that she thought I was in the sweet hereafter. She spoke to me in a hollow moan as though she were addressing spirits at a séance. Still, she called me daily, leaving messages when I didn't answer, assuring me not to worry, *he* would not get past her a second time.

Rock's voice was another on-going intrusion. Apparently, the authorities were not making headway in solving the crime. So why tell me about it? He must have thought I cared because of the mistaken identity schtick, which I knew was absurd. However, I had finally returned one of his incessant dragnet messages, mainly because I didn't want him breaking down the door and radically disturbing my concentration. Our connection had that otherworldly sound of the cell, the strange breaks while waiting for the message to be conveyed, as if it had to travel a long distance, reminding me again of my grandfather's shortwave radio. Yet, he was not far, in the dead woman's apartment, directly below me. I had the impression, confirmed by Schmidt, that he was always around, sneaking and snooping and listening. I felt sure that, like Columbo in the television series, he would eventually, seemingly inadvertently, outsmart his opponent.

Social scientists have tried to link writers to madness with little success.

Now that surprised me. If my contact with writers was typical, and I had no reason to believe it was not, I would have said that the link was fairly strong. But looking at it from another angle, it was good news, since once again I considered myself to be a writer. Once again, a seed of something inside me wanted to grow. Nourished by Harry, that is, the inspiration of his presence, I had batted out several pages of my prairie novel, if batting can describe a slow and painstaking progress. Still, I had a start.

Again, the buzzer. Would a canvasser keep trying? But I had no interest in seeing anyone. The past few days with Harry had been so wonderfully productive, so immensely satisfying, I did not want to be plunged back into the real world. Lying next to my landscape, my new found land, with the bedcovers between us of course (I didn't dare so much as stroke his cheek), my whole being filled, much like a balloon, with ideas that later showed up on my computer screen.

...seek inspiration at the bottom of the glass. Nature of the enterprise: eternally sitting at a desk feels less like the labour of an adult than the punishment of a child, who, while grounded, can only imagine the world going by.

It was then I heard a scraping, a scrabbling like the small claws of a small dog. I froze. Perhaps on the other side of the bedroom door Harry had made the sound. But, no, it came again and it was definitely from the door to the corridor. Someone must have let the buzzer in, in spite of warning notices and the recent murder.

I don't know how long I stayed frozen in uncomprehending consternation before I became aware of the rattling of a key in my lock. No, not a key, a tinny scratchy sound, someone was manipulating the lock with a wire. I got up, softly, I'm not sure why. I was not the intruder. I set down the newspaper, being careful not to rustle it, tiptoed into the kitchen and picked up the first thing that came to hand, a cast iron frying pan that was sitting on top of the stove. I arrived back just as the pseudo key was successful. The door inched open. The grain in the wood came alive with the intensity of my stare. I raised the pan high.

The head and shoulders of a man peeked around the half open door. We stared at each other a moment before both shouting in unison, "What are you doing here?"

Quickly following my first question came another. "Who are you?" And then, "You can't be ... you're not..." I lowered the pan.

Gully Jillson opened the door wider and dodged into the apartment, looking back over his shoulder into the corridor in a particularly evasive manner. He moved so quickly and I was so stunned, I did not have the time or inclination to protest. I could imagine how he had gotten into the building, shifting in behind a tenant or a legitimate visitor. He stood half crouched, a wizened creature in a shabby overcoat too large and a toque too small so that his wild grey hair straggled out from under it like an overflowing soufflé. His moustache had thawed into a limp greyish mop, long straggly strings of it covered his mouth. Several days growth grizzled the lower half of his face, over cheeks that had drunk the wind, to use the Yeatsian term. Eyeglasses and bushy eyebrows covered the top half. He was staring at me as if he were seeing a ghost.

"Do you mind if I sit down," he said in a voice like a rusty saw. "I've just had a terrible shock."

His eyes, with their haunted craziness, made me think of Dostoevsky's frenetic saints. He was trembling, as from nerves or alcohol, or maybe from the cold. My eyes fastened on a thin blue scarf. I had a moment of film noir – a man shows up at the door, camera pans to scarf, next scene, same scarf, only this time it's tight around the neck of a female victim lying sprawled on a rug. In true Hitchcockian style, I could see him doubled in the panel of mirror tiles beside the door. I tightened my grip on the frying pan.

"No. Yes. Yes, I do mind. You may not sit down," I stated emphatically. That may sound cruel for he had once been my husband, although in his case that was a minus not a plus. And he did seem on his last legs. But, after all, I was a frail helpless female and he looked like the sort of creature you might see digging in garbage cans on Ninth Avenue. And he was such a con artist, a true traveling salesman type – you let one foot in the door, the rest of him is in before you can say lickety-split, and you've just bought the Brooklyn bridge. I should not have even been standing there talking to him. He was wanted by the police.

"Leave. Immediately!" I raised the pan with one hand. I pointed toward the door with the other. I tried to stand tall. I tried to look robust.

With that, he gave me the piercing eye and pronounced, "You're dead."

He spoke with such conviction that, for an instant, I wondered if I might be in a parallel universe where everything has already happened.

"You're dead," he repeated, staring at me through those demented eyes magnified by prescription lenses. "The paper," he said. "Don't you read the paper?"

Our eyes travelled to the accumulated newspapers in the corner near the window. He scuttled over to the pile, riffled through it, found what he wanted and stuck it in my face. My vocal cords went into paralysis. I could only stare in dismay at the wet marks on my white carpet. "There, see that." He all but jumped in glee like the dwarf in the fairy tale.

"Death of second skier," the words danced before my eyes. "Name withheld pending notification of next of kin."

"Can you imagine what a shock it is," he said, "to have you rise from the dead. Like Lazarus."

"I was not dead," I said, in a daze.

"Where were you then?"

"They thought I was in Belize," I said without conviction.

"And were you?"

"No..."

"Well, then." He threw up his hands in disgust, as if to say, what can you expect when people are not where they're supposed to be.

"This isn't me," I intoned, throwing aside the newspaper. "There are so many accidents in the mountains. They all sound the same." Then it occurred to me, "What made you think it was me?" I looked at the man wavering before my eyes as he danced from one foot to the other like a child having to use the bathroom. I narrowed my eyes and looked at him more closely. Could this used up old man be the good-looking hunk I had married thirty-five years before? Could he be the successful novelist, pipe in hand, I had seen in a newspaper photograph no more than two years ago and in Sergeant Rock's hand a few weeks ago? Even more to the point, could he be the man who was the same age as me? I took a step backward. Maybe I had been mistaken. "Who *are* you?" I said trying to keep my voice even.

He grabbed onto a chair back which seemed to steady him. He regarded me, his eyes behind his spectacles, as my dear grandfather used to put it, like two pee holes in the snow. "Do you *really* not recognize me, Constance?" His voice was low, raspy. "Or are you playing one of your games?"

The way he said my name, his voice intimate, the way he knew my name, of course I recognized him. I also recognized that he would be up to something. "What happened?" I whispered, already suspicious of the answer.

His face screwed up something awful. He whimpered, "Oh, I know I'm a mess, but to think I've changed that much..." When he started to cry, my suspicion was verified. He had always pulled that one, the whole five years we were married. Any time he wanted something from me, he would put on the cry-baby act.

I consciously hardened my heart. This man is not your friend, I sternly reminded myself. Because of this man you have lost jobs, you have failed to get writing grants, you have had perfect strangers ring you up and rail at you over the phone.

Because we were married, people tended to think we were as one, same opinions, same principles and values. Nothing could have been further from the truth. He was always mouthing off and causing scenes, alienating and irritating people. His feuds with the literary mafia were famous, which did not reflect well on me. These were the people on hiring committees and literary boards. It was amazing the way gossip ran rampant in the arts community. It was amazing the way people put two and two together and got five.

In truth, Gully Jillson and I were as different as night and day. In the first place, he was male, I female. It's true that we were the same age and I guess we did have our writing in common, if you call all making of black marks on white paper writing. But he was a successful novelist who thought of his writing as a marketable commodity. My poems voiced a deeply felt sensibility mined with great effort from the very core of my being.

We were such opposites it was amazing that we had stayed married as long as we had. Gully was a man with a tremendous hunger for fame and fortune churning in his belly which, no doubt, explained, at least in part, his incredible ego-centredness. This self-absorption spilled over into everything he did. You want to hear what I wrote today, he would say immediately after sex. As you might guess, his prose was hard-driving and energetic. It was also a huge hit with the public, while my small volumes of sensitive poetry languished unread on library shelves and remainder tables. When I bitched about this, he said that my failure was my own fault, that if I'd get my ass together I could have my books leaping out of the remainder bins, I could get slots on talk shows, I could be invited on the rubber chicken reading circuit. But the sad fact is, we write what we must. I could not write the one-dimensional commercially successful novel even if I had wanted to, which I did not. Everything I wrote was ponderous and meaningful. The fact that no one was interested in my deep sensibility was not a primary concern. I was satisfying my own need for expression.

Gully had stopped crying and was looking at me intently. "You're a fine one to talk," he was starting to bristle for battle, "you're no hell yourself."

I felt a moment of insult before considering where the remark had come from. Over the years, I had kept myself trim, still had my own teeth, wore spectacles only when I wanted to see, still had gobs of hair, curly blonde, thanks to the blessings of the bottle. I believed my face was still somewhat attractive taking into consideration its age. It was a nervous sensitive face with full lips and hazel eyes. People told me that I looked considerably younger than my years. So what did I care what a smelly old reprobate thought of me. "Some people think I look fine," I retorted. "The people who matter."

"Don't believe them," he said. "You look terrible. A scrawny chicken. And what's that bush you've got on top of your head? Why do you insist on being a phony bleached blonde? Grey is much more attractive. It goes with the wrinkles."

I looked at that poor pathetic being who was fouling the air of the room. I remembered then that people used to say we looked alike. They joked about it – how many couples start to look alike after they've been married a long time, but we started out looking alike. If that was true, and I wasn't saying it was, we did it in reverse. I don't look like him now, I decided with relief. I could see some basic resemblance, all right – high cheekbones, square face, wide-set eyes. We both had hair that stood out all around our heads. I didn't have a moustache, although I suppose I could have had, the way I had been tweaking those hairs on my chin and upper lip the last couple of years, misguided hormones according to the magazine articles. But life had ravaged us each in different ways. Gully's destruction was external and obvious but I knew it could not be deep, because he was not a deep person. On the other hand, although people continued to tell me how well I looked even as I headed for the mountain, inside I was a ruined city, one that had been sacked and pillaged and burned to ashes.

I did feel some pity at the change in Gully since the last newspaper article. When had it appeared in our local paper? I couldn't remember. God, my memory was becoming abysmal. It was after he'd done the Wild Bill thing. The Wild Bill stories appeared when I was still on the ranch with my children. I would read those stories to Lara and we would paste them in her scrapbook with all the other stories about her father. That was when I was a mother, writing for pleasure, not taking it or myself too seriously. When I was out of love with Harry and not yet in love with the one-armed ranch hand. When I was content. When I was happy. I felt sadness for both of us and the passing of time.

"What do you want?" I glared.

"What do you mean?" His eyes shifted to one side of the room.

"You always want something."

"That's not true."

"It is true. Why can't you tell the truth for a change? Everybody knows you're a pathological liar."

"I suppose you're still sore about that girl ... I never pretended to be perfect."

"No, you certainly didn't."

"I was drunk."

"You certainly were."

"Lots of men stray. Statistics show that sixty percent of married men have affairs."

The last time I'd had anything to do with Gully except through lawyers was at a party in a Toronto hotel room after his acceptance speech for the Governor General's award. When I went to retrieve my coat from an adjoining room, I noticed the pile moving, rhythmically. When I dug under, there he was with some bimbo, her legs wrapped around him. I marched with as great a dignity as I could muster out of the hotel room. The rest is history. The GG opened enough doors for him so that even with his mediocre powers as a novelist, he was a huge success. His comic novels involving pathetic characters tormented by the misapplication of their genitalia were gobbled up by the public. Then, gearing himself for a wider market, and perhaps encouraged in this by his publisher, he transferred to the wild west. While his cowboy novels retained a comic tone (there was an ongoing grizzled old-timer in the manner of Gabby Hayes of old Hollywood western fame), they contained a thick layer of sex for the female audience and violence for the men. As might be expected, his characters were always shallow stereotypes. His forte was a powerful story structure on which to hang character and setting. He'd found a gimmick and made it work for him, and in that way, I had to admit he was talented. Ever the showman, he reinvented himself as the quintessential western hero, Wild Bill Hickok, and rode the wild west show circuit for several years. All this, I got from newspapers and journals. After the split, I'd had nothing more to do with Gully, even though we had a daughter in common. But he never knew about that.

So here he was, my nemesis, in defeat, head hanging forward, thawed moustache dripping on my white broadloom, blubbering and making no attempt to cover his face. I should have been pleased. I wasn't. Why did I feel that his defeat was mine?

"Oh, for heaven's sake," I said, knowing as I said it that I was making a mistake. "Sit down. Here," I reached into the pocket of my robe and brought out a wad of tissue. By then I had set down the frying pan. "Blow your nose."

He blew as directed. "How can you be so horrid," he whined, sinking onto the sofa. "You know you're the one I truly cared for." This coming from a man who had been married I don't know how many times, I'd lost count, to say nothing of several torrid relationships that blazed a path through the literary arts sections of the papers.

"Forget it," I said. "Past history. I don't care any more. Just tell me what you want then I'll say 'no', then you can leave."

"Couldn't I have wanted to see you?

"You thought I was dead."

God bless him, it took him only a second to recover. "I had to see for myself."

"You've seen. Now go!"

"Come on Constance, don't be so mean. Can't we let bygones be bygones?"

"Me, mean! You invade my privacy with your smarmy presence, wanting something as usual, and you call me mean! Do you forget that you destroyed my life?"

"I didn't destroy your life." His red tear-stained eyes took a wild swing around the room. "You wouldn't happen to have something to drink around the place, would you?"

I ignored the request. "What do you call it when a person steals another person's novel?"

"I didn't steal your novel." His voice had lost its wheedling tone and was now definitely aggressive. It wouldn't be long before he became his old pompous, supercilious self and I became the intruder in my own apartment.

"You stole my idea."

"You can't copyright an idea."

"That's no excuse. And how about characters and plot line? Common decency should have kept you from using my plot line. Oh, but then I forget, you never did possess that valuable commodity."

"I can't believe you're still hung up on that silly old novel. You would never have gotten it written. You let everything and everybody distract you from your work. I wrote it in six weeks."

My eyeballs felt like they would pop out of my head in an apoplectic fit. The reason I could not have got it written in six weeks was because I was cooking his meals, popping beer caps for his writing buddies, and hauling the empties to the recycling depot. I even brought him coffee on a tray to his study. Of course, I didn't know then what he was writing. "If you recall, those were the days I was waiting on you hand and foot," I screeched. I couldn't help it.

"You could have refused to wait on me. No, Connie, you're a procrastinator, pure and simple."

"No matter how you try and get around it, the fact is you got me drunk that night and conned me into showing you the first draft. You then won the GG with it. What would you call that?"

"Genius. I took a blob of clay and turned it into a masterpiece."

"Masterpiece, my foot. You turned it into a one-dimensional bestseller. My draft was about the importance of landscape to forge identity, my draft plumbed the depths of the human condition…"

"Your draft was unreadable. I worked like hell to shape it into some sort of coherent form. Oh, I'll admit I got some of the ideas from you, but the finished book bore no resemblance to your draft. I worked hard on that book. I wrote the goddamn thing, not you. If you'd get your head out of your ass and stop writing silly poetry, you could write a bestseller too."

I knew from experience that there was no sense arguing with him. He always could twist everything around and make it look like I was in the wrong. When you meet the devil, turn tail and start walking as fast as you can. So goes the advice of the experts. Since we were in my apartment, I couldn't do that. But I could do the next best thing.

"Get out!" Feet planted, hands on hips, drawing myself up to my five-foot-two, I shouted it.

"I read your book," he quickly interjected.

"Which book."

"The last one. I forget its name. It was great."

"You don't read poetry."

"I don't usually. But I did yours."

It occurred to me to challenge him with a quiz about the book. But, then he would have been successful in diverting my attention off topic. "I want you to leave this minute," I said. "You're not supposed to be here."

"Neither are you," he shot back. "How would you feel if someone you thought was dead turned out to be alive?"

"I might be relieved."

"Well, of course, I'm relieved. But it's still a shock."

"Anyway," I clipped my tone and frosted my delivery, "whether I'm alive or dead is irrelevant. The question is, since you thought I was dead, what are you doing here?"

"I couldn't believe it. I had to see for myself. You have no idea what a turn it gave me. It was like *I* was no longer in the world. It made me realize the deep bond that exists between us, in spite of everything. It made me realize that we belong together."

"Oh? So where have you been the last thirty years."

"I've been busy. You have no idea … readings, book signings, promotion. Publishers are so demanding. But you were always in my mind. My place is with you and you know it."

"Bullshit. Get out!"

"Have you looked out the window lately? Here you are cocooned in your safe little world. How about the rest of us who have to go out into the storm?"

"Get out!" By now I was shouting.

"But you always were like that. You never did face reality. Life for you is the fetal position. No wonder you never got any place with your writing."

"At least I haven't ended up like you."

"Look, this is more important than our petty squabbling." He held out his unsteady hands in supplication. "He's back."

Suddenly, everything became clear. I knew why Gully was here. I knew why he had been in the building the night of the murder, why, in Schmidt's words, he had been skulking *furtively.* I decided to play dumb, as the detective stories put it. "Who's back?"

"You know."

"I don't know. I don't know what you're talking about."

"What would I be talking about? What other subject is there?"

He snatched up the newspaper that had fallen onto the coffee table and thrust it in my hands. "While the dead skier has not yet been identified, the man buried to his neck in the avalanche and subsequently dug out by Air Services Rescue has been identified as Harry Weinstein."

I lowered the paper slowly until only my eyes were peering over the top. Gully's red-rimmed subterranean orbs met mine with a chilling impersonal stare.

"No," I said.

"I just thought..."

"No," I repeated.

"The hospital discharged him two weeks ago. He must be some place."

"Why don't you ask at the hospital."

"They won't give out information to anyone who isn't family."

I looked at the man before me in the shabby coat and filthy toque that he might have plucked out of someone's garbage. Was this a costume to wheedle his way back into my life and to try and get at Harry through me? This man was a well-rehearsed actor, a man who would stop at nothing to create a powerful, if fake, identity; a man who would put on any mask to get what he wanted.

"Maybe he doesn't want to be found, doesn't want to be bothered by the likes of you. He's getting old too. He's older than we are. Maybe he can't take it any more."

"He'd want to see me. You know that."

"I know no such thing." I thought quickly. I must deflect Gully from the scent. I must get him out of here. If he suspected something, I'd never get rid of him. "I believe he has some relatives somewhere. Maybe he's with them. Or with his latest amour."

"No, I've checked around. He's disappeared into thin air."

There was a pause in which I found myself staring at his clasped hands. The knuckles had become large, especially those of the thumbs, which seemed disjointed from his hands. Only last year, I had noticed the knuckles of my own hands had become larger. I felt myself starting to feel pity. No, I cried to myself. No, no. Don't do it!

"I guess you may as well know," he said, "things haven't been going well for me. I haven't had a book out for five years."

"I did read something."

"I never thought it would happen to me."

I sank wearily onto the couch. For a moment I wondered if perhaps I *was* dead. I felt so impotent in the face of the bludgeoning aspects of life. Every time I got going, every time I was on the brink of achievement, the hard drive went belly up or the freezer died quietly in the night leaving me with a thawed side of beef and no one to cook for. Then there were the more serious catastrophes, a child falling off a horse, a parent dying, a friend getting cancer. Now, just when I had Harry secured in my bed, just when I was doing so well with my quintessential prairie novel, who should show up but Gully Jillson intoning in a sorrowful voice, "I can't get it up any more."

I knew what he meant – the dreaded affliction, the curse every writer feared: Writer's Block.

"I need to find him, to talk," Gully continued.

"Maybe he's too sick to talk."

"That's just it, I have to talk to him before he goes and dies on me."

I looked at him, I hoped long and hard. His remark was *so* Gully. "You really don't care about anybody else, do you, just so long as you get *your* book out. You'd sell your own mother down the river."

"Hey, no need to get mean. No need to blame other people for *your* failure. You know what your big problem is? Your fatal flaw, as you like to call it?"

"My fatal flaw is that I put up too long with assholes like you."

"No, that's not it at all, Connie. I'm gonna tell you what it is."

"I don't wish to hear your stupid opinion."

"I'm going to tell you anyway. You don't care whether you win or lose. That was the problem in our marriage. It's no fun playing with someone who doesn't care. I can't stand playing with a person who doesn't care."

"Tell someone who cares."

"So now you're going to do dog in a manger." His voice was becoming nasty, the way it could, as I clearly remembered. "You're going to keep something from me that I need when I could make good use of it and you can't. It was the same way with your novel. You had a big mess of words there, baby. You never would've made head nor tail out of that muddle. I did something with it. We're back at square one. You still don't know how to make use of what's in front of your nose."

"I'll give you some money to tide you over," I said, "but I don't want to ever see you again."

"I don't need money. I need a place to stay."

"No."

"Just for a few days. So I can catch my breath."

"Definitely not. No way."

"You can't send me away. What kind of person would send another person out into a blizzard. You wouldn't send a dog out in this."

"A dog didn't ruin my life."

"Please, Connie. You don't need to be afraid of me. I'm

battered. I'm finished. I'm like a salmon that's been swimming upstream. Life has dealt me too many blows. I just need a place to recuperate, maybe die."

His theatrical pleading made me think of the man in the picture, the one with the twirly moustache and deerskin shirt, the actor, the phony.

But something else occurred to me. "What made you think I was that dead skier?"

"What do you mean?" His eyes slid sideways.

"You know what I mean. They didn't publish a name."

"It sounded like you."

"How did you know I'd gone skiing?" My voice went up a notch. "You were here weren't you? You saw the ski brochures on the coffee table." We both looked toward the pile of glossy travel folders that were still stacked on the table where I had left them nearly a month ago. "You snooped on my desk. You looked at my calendar. You looked in my storeroom for my skis. You've been touching *my* stuff!"

"Now, wait a minute..."

"The police are looking for you."

At that, the worry lines in his forehead increased. His eyes became even more frantic. He held his breath. "What for?"

"A woman in the building was murdered. The same night you were breaking into my apartment. Someone saw you leaving the building."

He let out his breath. "We both know that's crazy."

"Yes," I said, for I now knew what had happened. Gully had, even then, been looking for Harry.

"C'mon Connie. Don't be cross. We had some good times though, didn't we? We had a lot of fun together. Jesus but we had fun. Remember when we met? Those crazy times with Harry? That winter writing retreat at Banff?" Gully was pulling out the emotional stops. His ammunition was memory. We had meant something to each other in the past. Our lives together spanned a lifetime. Even if we hadn't seen each other for most of it, we had existed all those long years in each other's minds. But it wasn't that that made me change my mind when he pressed on, "C'mon. Be a sport."

I would have to be careful. I would have to be very careful that he did not catch on about Harry. I had to think up a plan. While I did that, I had a better chance of keeping an eye on him if he was under my roof and thumb. Otherwise, his attack could come from anywhere at any time.

"I'll give you exactly three days to rest up, then toodle-oo." My voice was emphatic. "You can have the spare room and you must stay there, except for meals. I have no intention of preparing same. I'll take mine in my room. The bedrooms in this apartment have individual locks. My bedroom door will always be locked. I'm going there right now, I can feel a migraine coming on."

"Before you go…"

"What?" I scowled and snapped.

"Is there anything to eat around here? I'm starved"

Before I could splutter a reply, he capered over to the door and opened it. Swiftly and adroitly, he plucked a suitcase from where it was stashed in the corridor, while my eyes widened with horror at the sight of another rust-coloured mark on the white carpet where he had been standing.

5.

⊸⟶⟍⟋⟵⊷

THE CURTAIN RISES ON THE LIVING ROOM of my apartment. The furniture is as previously placed – long white sofa before window, white chairs at either end, purchased at a time when I regarded white as inspiring rather than terrifying and had not got around to changing. The coffee table is of chrome and glass, travel brochures artistically fanned for display purposes. The large windows are undraped. White flakes swirl against the glass, doubling in the mirror tiles on the opposite wall turning the room into a snow globe. The tasteful, austere, interior decorating is that of a minimalist stage set upon which the play will be enacted without benefit of distracting trappings. The words, the wit, are what will count.

This is the moment just before the start of the action, a moment of stasis, even harmony, which invites, which insists upon, its own destruction.

Two weeks had passed since Gully's appearance, two days becoming two weeks, which, let's face it, was inevitable. Of course he would wheedle for an extension. Of course, I would give in. He made sure he was the perfect guest, silent and invisible. We had settled into an edgy truce. He was installed in the spare room down the hall with instructions not to come out except for food and drink and use of bathroom facilities. The new deal was he had six weeks to write a blockbuster bestseller that would set him back on his feet. The negotiations that led to that outcome I have omitted. The attempt in this dissertation is for coherency rather than lunacy. Reluctantly, I had supplied him with a key to the apartment. At the same time, I added a dead bolt to the catch lock on my bedroom door. Naturally, he was free to come and go as he wished, so long as such exits and entrances were quietly accomplished. Unlike the great poet Weyman Chan, who was able to compose while sitting in the Food Fair in a shopping mall, I needed absolute quiet when I was involved in the act of creation.

Rock had not left a message for several days but, according to the spies, he was still in the building, which came as no surprise. Although I could not see him, I could feel his presence, hovering in the corridor, checking out the utility closets, asking questions in the apartments of other tenants. I felt uneasy. Why was he hanging around? Surely he had gotten everything out of the building and its inhabitants there was to get. Did he still want to question Gully? I had to admit to myself that the blood on Gully's shoe, which he transferred to the carpet, was suspicious. But was it blood? Down on my hands and knees a second time, diligently rubbing, I decided that my imagination was working overtime. My mind was still adamant that the father of my daughter could not commit such a deed. What would be the motive? He swore that he had never been in the eleventh floor apartment. I could not check out his shoes; at my instruction he had wiped them clean. I could not question him further. Every time I considered a confrontation, I shied back, like a horse will when it sees a rattlesnake on the trail. I kept telling myself I would ask him tomorrow and tomorrow and tomorrow.

As for Rock, he did not know about Gully but he knew about Harry. He and Missing Persons and naturally the hospital were the only ones who did know. I had smuggled Harry into the apartment in the dead of night, with only the help of the ambulance paramedics, quite amusing because he almost fell off the narrow stretcher. But that's another story. As to this story, I had to be very careful to keep Harry's presence in my bed a secret, and it wasn't only Gully I had to watch out for. If the literary crowd got wind of Harry, they would be swarming up here like locusts. He had a lot of friends in this town, a lot of disciples and devotees. I would not stand a chance against the horde.

These worries, needless to say, were causing me a whole lot of anxiety, and it was only with a great deal of mental effort I was able to put them on the back burner, so to speak. Thank heavens, Aunt Olive understood my need for solitude when creating and did not phone except to tell me that if I had any sense at all I'd invite Rock in for coffee. Schmidt phoned but was willing to leave messages, mainly warning me to keep my door locked.

And so with all distractions settled satisfactorily, I settled down to write.

I cocooned myself in my room. I did not wish to run into Gully in the kitchen, or anywhere else for that matter. However, much to my dismay, after the surge of optimism inspired by taking to my side of the bed with Harry, after my party of one interrupted by Gully, nothing was emerging. After the high of inspiration, the low of perspiration set in. I could not enact the actual sitting down and tackling the task. When I lay beside Harry, staring at his face, white as the pillow beneath his head, knowing he was dreaming of prairie landscape, trying to share in that landscape for my quintessential prairie novel, I could not make our minds as one. I tried connecting our mental images – black telephone wires spanning a long landscape of snow – tried letting speechless vibes flow in and out, into me from him, out from me onto the page. But it was no use. Things were at a standstill. I could only force out weak little dribbles at long and irregular intervals.

Oh, I sat down every day. I knew the rule on that one. But instead of writing I found myself listening for the sounds of another in the apartment – the thud of a door being closed,

the flush of a toilet, the gush of a tap, the soft shuffle of footsteps into the kitchen. All I heard was silence interrupted by
the occasional dry hacking coughing fit of the smoker. What
the hell was he doing? Why wasn't he opening and closing
the fridge door? He was thin as a rail, he should be eating. It
twigged. He had not bought groceries. Why didn't he go out
and buy groceries? If that wasn't just like him.

He had always been like that. On a writing binge, he would
forget to eat. And he was definitely on a binge. After the first
few days of silence, one of which was taken up by installing a
computer, a veritable stream of tapping came from the spare
room. When I made forays into the kitchen for food and passed
by his door – it was only a few steps out of my way – when
I stopped and bent my ear to the wood, I could hear a faint
rhythm of fingers on a keyboard.

He was producing, while I, cloistered in my room, condemned
to my chair, nodding off before the screen, was becoming
increasingly annoyed with the lifeless man in my bed, the comatose head on the pillow. Harry had always been moody but
this was going too far. Goddammit! I found myself cursing.
Why had he put himself in my way if all he was going to do
was lie there?

I saw to it that he had all the amenities. I waited on him hand
and foot, adjusting him daily to prevent bed sores, changing
his intravenous drip, sponging the parts of him I could get at,
his old flabby chest, the loose skin of his arms, remembering
the fine figure of a man he had once been.

What was he afraid of? It was not like I was making unreasonable demands, for Christ's sake. Wimp! Why didn't he
stand up and respond like a man? He was supposed to respond.
That was in the script given me by the hospital nurse and the
doctor who had signed his release form. His vital signs are
responsive, they said. What he needs now is constant loving
home care. The home nurse who visited weekly, during which
time I turned the key from the outside in the spare room lock,

announced that he was doing fine. He'll come out of it, she predicted. When? I asked. When he's ready, she answered. While I was supposed to be writing, these thoughts chased each other through my head until my eyes glazed and my head fell forward and hit the keyboard. I looked up quickly to see what keys I had inadvertently activated. Nothing, not even a message that I had performed an illegal operation and would be shut down immediately.

Oh hell, I wasn't getting anywhere. I figured I may as well go out and get some groceries for Gully. I needed a few things anyway. I closed my screen, made sure I locked my door, quietly removed my coat from the closet, then had to find my purse. I had a bad habit of leaving it lying about. This time it was in the kitchen, on top of the fridge. I grabbed it, made sure I had my charge card, crept out and returned an hour later with seven plastic bags suspended from stretched ligaments. I transferred all contents into fridge and cupboard and tapped lightly on Gully's door. "Bananas," I said, having remembered while going through the bins at Safeway that when writing he ate gobs of bananas for quick energy.

Having taken care of the grocery problem, I settled down once more to write.

Over the next several days, everything that did not require preparation disappeared. Bread, cheese, pickles, cold cuts – all gone. I spotted empty precooked sausage packaging in the garbage and no evidence of pot or plate, knife or fork. One day he had gone so far as to open a tin of brown beans, the remains of which were on the counter along with the can opener. It was then I wondered about doing some cooking, just one meal daily. No. No. No, I screamed to myself. Stop it! Right this minute!

While Gully tipped and tapped away, I became increasingly engrossed in the act of sleeping in my swivel chair. I simply could not stay awake. Neither could my computer. I would jolt alert to the black screen, where I was confronted by a stranger only to realize a moment later that I was looking at my own reflection.

Night was another matter. In an attempt to facilitate vibes, I had moved permanently from cot to bed. I would place myself carefully on top of the covers, heedful of Harry's tubes, careful not to jostle him or the paltry pages of my writing that had accumulated on his side of the bed. I figured that since Harry never moved a muscle and since there was an eighteen-inch gap between him and the edge of the bed, I might as well utilize that space for organizing my files.

There I lay, straight and still, through the long hours, staring at the dark ceiling as though it were yet another frustrating computer screen. I tried to utilize the time by working out some plot complication or character development. Instead my mind would float and settle on past slights and humiliations, the reviewer of my last collection ten years ago who was tired of reading about the prairie and homesteaders eating gopher to stay alive. Why, I raged to the dark, if you totally lack professional objectivity and are abysmally ignorant of the subject material, why would you even attempt to review my poems, you asshole brain-deficient moron, you supercilious ego-swollen undergraduate English major?

Adrenalin pumping, heart pounding, I would, very carefully, slide myself to the edge of the bed, slowly swing my legs around, stand up and go to the kitchen where I made myself a bracing coffee. To hell with decaf. I needed something to calm my nerves. I sat at the kitchen table and listened to Gully's muffled taps down the hall. Did the guy never sleep? One night he was silent. That was the night I saw a blur at the side of my vision. I remembered that I hadn't bothered to lock my door. I quickly turned my head. But it was only one of those tricks of the eye. Paranoid whacko, I muttered to myself and lit another cigarette.

I could not blame Gully for my state. He was behaving himself. He was following my instructions to a T. He seemed to be taking seriously my six-week ultimatum. I remembered that he had always been disciplined about his work – first thing every morning he would write his daily quota, two finished pages. To facilitate my time deadline, he had cooperatively upped his current output to six.

Filling the tea kettle at the kitchen sink, I found myself wondering what had happened. Why hadn't he had a bestseller or even a book for several years now? Maybe it had been the women, the public, the friends who kept him out all night boozing because *they* didn't want to face the blank page. Maybe fame and fortune had been too much for him. But the Gully of old would still have done his two pages every day. No matter what else was on his agenda, in his first three waking hours he got those two pages done, unlike me who could spend three hours rearranging a comma in a poem. To all intents and purposes, he lived a twenty-one hour day and fit life, what other people thought of as life, into that. And those around him had to understand. If they did not, too bad, been good to know you. When I knew him, no one was ever allowed to overstep that particular rule. No one. That was his writing strength. That was his human weakness.

Something must have shattered that discipline. I had heard rumours – the last woman had given *him* the boot, he had invested money into a project that had failed, he had started doing cocaine – but so many rumours float about in the literary domain. And I knew that none of those things in themselves would have got to him. He would shrug off a failed relationship and go on to the next one. He would never put a drug habit before his work. Work was the driving force in his life. As long as I can work, I'm okay, that's what he used to say. Something, then, must have happened which interfered with his work, something that caused a failure of his imaginative will. His muse had deserted him. But who or what was his muse? I had been married to the guy, yet I didn't know. In interviews and on talk shows he did not seem to mind discussing other intimate details of his life, but he was very close on the subject of muses. In fact, he spoke scathingly of muses as being romantic mumbo jumbo. What inspires you to write? was an often-asked question. Money, was his answer, always with a little chuckle to clue the audience in to his little joke of undermining his own great genius.

Well, money was certainly a serious subject for him at the moment. And he *was* working like a madman. How could he recover from his block so readily while my screen remained blank? I caught myself. Envy was a destructive emotion that could cause paralysis. Thou shalt not envy: I repeated it over and over to myself.

But maybe I *could* blame my writer's block on Gully. Maybe another presence in the apartment was interfering with Harry's vibes, rather like electrical interference. Or maybe Gully's presence down the hall had its own vibes, destructive vibes, which were affecting me, which were stronger than Harry's constructive vibes. Maybe Gully's presence was bringing back old hurtful episodes that I had trained myself not to think about. Why cause myself pain when it could be avoided, I had reasoned. Why think about how you loved your children, how they grew up and went away and how that happy time in your life seemed to have happened to another person. Why think about how you throw your little book out into the world, a lamb to the slaughter of ignorance and stupidity.

I did not want my whole life coursing through me like a never-ending reel of anguish, humiliation, and regret. As far as the real world was concerned, I liked being shallow.

Was that what Lara had meant? When she heard about the death of my last husband, she phoned me from down east where she was attending university. As luck would have it, I could not remember the man's name. It was one of those mental lapses we are all subject to, especially under stress, but Lara didn't miss the opportunity to fire away. "You're so careless, the way you mislay husbands and children and friends. The way you refuse to name anything, to pin anything down, you have no depth, no emotional sensitivity."

Maybe so, but it had got me through the last decade of writing articles on safe subjects – lattice garden dividers and pioneer museums. Now that I had taken it into my head to write something of a more profound nature, I couldn't write anything at all.

I did put something down one day – *how good a job did you do with the people, the minds that were entrusted to you in this life?* I quickly deleted it and took to my bed beside Harry.

An expression of disgust turned down his lips. I knew I was hallucinating. Still, with a huge sigh of anguish at the unfairness of things, I dragged myself back up and over to my swivel chair. I resumed staring. Maybe I should get myself a coffee. No, my stomach already hurt. How about a muffin? I looked at my watch. Eleven-thirty. I supposed I could have lunch, except sometime during the last three hours I had already consumed lunch, as well as breakfast and dinner. I vaguely recalled shuffling into the kitchen, slowly, mechanically, chewing a muffin, then an hour later, finding myself at the sink eating a tomato, some lettuce, a half slice of bread, then still later, ice cream straight from the carton. I remembered Raymond Chandler's advice about making yourself sit at your typewriter for four hours. You don't have to write during that time but you can't do anything else, either. You'll find yourself so bored you'll write something.

Sorry Ray, it doesn't work for some people. I sat there so long my computer developed a click which reminded me of my second last husband who kept clearing his throat and emitting little coughs. I firmly believe those are the things that break up marriages – the three regulated sneezes in a row, so that after the first one you tense for the second. It is only when the third has been accomplished that you can relax back in your chair. When the affair happens or the abuse or whatever, it is not the cause of the breakup but only a manifestation of a relationship in which both parties have irritated each other beyond their limits.

In spite of that rheumatic click, I was determined to get something done. I picked up a magazine from the clutter on my desk, flipped it open and randomly began to read. *Your passionate nature needs to be fulfilled*, the words floated into my consciousness. There it was in black and white on the monthly horoscope page. Your passionate nature needs to be fulfilled.

I turned my head toward the bed. The man lying there was not, definitely not, fulfilling my passionate nature. I thought about pulling the plug, finishing off for once and forever this stupid one-way relationship that should never have started in the first place. I sat very still. Was he still breathing? My own breathing was like the last scene in *Space Odyssey 2001*, the pulse of the universe, the pulse of humanity about to be born. I thought of all the breathing that had taken place since the beginning of time. I thought of the necessity of breathing. I became disproportionately conscious of my breath. In, out. In, out. I began to panic. Breathing, when you thought about it, is a terrible responsibility. Breathing was something my body had to do every day of my life, an unconscious choice of my mind. I became totally overwhelmed with the task of breathing. I couldn't breathe. Panic took over.

At that very moment, the doorbell rang. I jumped. Blessed relief. I didn't care who it was – Amway, Jehovah's Witnesses, encyclopedia salesman. But it was more likely Aunt Olive or Schmidt, one wanting me to lure Rock into my lair, the other wanting me to avoid him. I scurried into the living room, with all the hope and energy of one who has been delivered from a fate worse than death. I flung open the door. In the corridor stood the filthiest young woman I had ever seen. She looked and smelled as if she had been sleeping in a garbage dumpster. Her long tangled hair, the colour of which I could not make out, her jeans, her open coat, all was encrusted with grime. Through earphones clamped to her ears, I could hear the discordant notes of punk rock. Her face wore the vacant expression of those who are listening to music only they can hear. My eyes travelled down her length to toe rings embedded in ridges of accumulated dirt. Her toenails shone a brilliant green like the underbellies of ten little evil flies.

"Where're your boots!" I shrieked. "It's forty below outside!" She must have seen me gesticulating. She turned toward me. She took the plugs from her ears. She shuffled closer, with a query in her eyes, those startling blue eyes I remembered from her childhood, eyes which demanded truth and gave it back in return.

"Where are your boots?" I repeated, my voice still in the upper register.

"Oh, Mom, chill out. I left them in the foyer." Her voice was lower, quieter, more modulated than I remembered. It was the voice of a nurse in a psychiatric ward attempting to calm down a patient.

"You mean you came all the way through the foyer and up the elevator like that!" I nearly choked. How had she gotten past Schmidt? Obviously, the latter had not been at her desk, likely off playing detective.

"They were incredibly filthy. There's construction going on outside, in case you don't know. I didn't want to get the carpets dirty. You always used to yell at me about the carpets."

"I never yelled at you about the carpets!" I suddenly remembered Gully down the hall. I envisioned him with ears perked up. "I might have discussed the problem with you," I said in a lowered voice, "but I did not yell."

"Have it your way." Her voice clearly indicated that she was finding the discussion boring. "I remember you yelled."

Since there was no use pursuing this line of remembrance of things past, as I well knew, having engaged in this sort of thing ad nauseam when she was younger, I changed the subject. "Did anyone see you? Get in here. Close the door."

It was only then that I noticed an errant dodger hovering behind her.

"What's that?" I couldn't quite see because of the light in the corridor and the fact that I was wearing my reading glasses.

Lara moved aside, revealing a smallish person with a hump on his back. "I'd like you to meet Rowlf. Rowlf, this is my mother. I've told you about her."

Rowlf had spiked bright green and dark red hair, earrings all along his ear lobes, a staple in his eyelid. He was removing the hump that turned out to be a guitar, along with his coat, an act that revealed a black T-shirt. His arms were tattooed from wrist to shoulder. He was a squat creature – his legs seemed disproportionately short. He was equally filthy as Lara. He put forth a tentative hand that I pretended not to see.

"Rowlf was a fellow worker at the commune," Lara was saying.

Why would they come here from California this time of year? I wondered. Things seemed dark indeed.

"We did the cooking," Lara went on.

My God! They had been preparing food for a large group of people. No wonder we had Mad Cow and West Nile and SARS and AIDS. The world was indeed going to hell in a hand basket.

Just as I had always believed that when a piece of my writing was published, it was no longer mine but belonged to the world – I had also believed that I had a duty to release my children into the world. I had regarded with disdain and pity those who tied their children to them with emotional hanging rope. I recognized that young people would not attain true maturity unless they could break free of the chains of childhood. It was the right of all individuals to leave home, have adventures, kill the dragon, return triumphant.

I had reaped that whirlwind with a vengeance. Apart from a few brief visits, I had not seen this daughter for years. At the age of eighteen, she had gone east to pursue studies at a university in Toronto. Summers and between semesters she was occupied with jobs and projects. I was occupied with raising her younger brothers. During our last phone call, a year previous, she had told me that she was in California, that she had found a group of people who were now her family, that she was very happy and that she hoped I would understand.

I looked at my child. Lara had been the sweetest, cutest, cleanest little darling you ever did see. She never got dirty. She didn't *like* getting dirty. If she got jam on her fingers, "mommy, off," she'd say in her sweet baby voice. If she got dirt or sand on herself at the playground, she would run home crying. Surely, she was redeemable. All I had to do was bring her in and give her a good wash.

Hold on, I said to myself. This *child* is thirty years old. Besides, do you want to be thrown back to being a mother? Isn't that what you left with a sigh of relief so that finally you could get your writing done? In a flash like a video rewind, I saw all those years of frustrated creativity, years when I would be on the verge of a wonderful sentence, an amazing original thought, a fantastic image, and the fridge door would slam and I would jump up immediately before whoever it was consumed everything I had planned for dinner.

I looked at my child and realized that I did not know her any more. And she did not know me. There were great gaps between us where we had lost the details of each other's lives, great shadowy gaps in which she had grown from girl to woman, in which I had grown into early old age, or late middle age, whichever category the current demographic would place me. I had learned that there are moments in lives, times when you go through the dangerous mountain pass from one valley to the next, times when you transit the valley of affliction, and unless the other person has shared the journey with you as your companion along the way, you have missed each other – tragically, in the case of family. What hope for us is there? I asked myself miserably.

I looked at this young woman who had come out of my body thirty years ago. I had not been the best mother in the world, but I had done the best I could under the circumstances. Until she was five, I had been a single parent. There's no need to go into the unique set of problems that status entails. At age eighteen, she chose to go east to study, a choice I applauded – she needed to leave home and learn a thing or two about life. She insisted forever after that I had thrown her out into the world, which was not true, but whatever the case, it appeared that, after several years, the world had given up and thrown her back.

Still, she was my child. I stepped aside. Lara entered my pristine apartment. Rowlf shuffled in behind her. That person was not my child. "Stop where you are," I commanded. "Strip to your underwear. Both of you. I'll get a green garbage bag."

"Mom, you're being both ridiculous and insulting," Lara started. "What right do you have to comment on my chosen lifestyle?"

We looked each other in the eye, but I was resolved not to budge. I could not, I simply could not, give up what I had fought for so long and hard, the beautiful order and clean lines of my life, grace in a world rife with chaos. Her eyes fell first. She dropped her backpack; I made sure it landed on the plastic mat. But other matters were prominent in my mind, mainly, that it was not like Lara to capitulate without a fight. Something must be terribly wrong.

Lara started to unbutton her shirt. "You," I ordered Rowlf, "turn around."

"It's okay, Mom," Lara was skinning down her jeans, bending to remove them from her legs. "We're married."

At that I had to sit down.

"No..." I protested through numb lips.

"In a balloon." She dropped the jeans on the floor.

"That doesn't count."

"Yes it does. We signed something. It was fun, except Rowlf threw up."

"Vertigo," explained Rowlf, from where he was facing the window. "I never could take heights."

"And he was thoughtful enough to do it over the side. Weren't you sweetie?" With that she turned to Rowlf and stroked the back of his neck. Her face took on a pleasant aspect, the first since her arrival.

I realized that I was sitting on somebody's filthy backpack. I sprung up and got a plastic bag. After stuffing every bit of Lara's clothing into it, "you're next," I said across my shoulder to Rowlf.

As I marched Lara off to the bathroom, I felt that I was being involuntarily returned to being a mother with all the messiness that entailed. What hope that Harry would speak now, I mourned, but it seemed I had no choice.

6.

———— ∞∞∞ ————

"NOT ANOTHER DEPRESSING PRAIRIE NOVEL," protested Aunt Olive, tossing my painfully conceived and carefully contrived three pages onto the middle of my kitchen table where they lay awash in a puddle of coffee.

Quickly, I retrieved them.

"During the three-day journey, Jenny's spirits fell in direct proportion to the nearness of her destination," I read out loud. "As the wheels clicked and clacked across the wide expanse of unbroken flatness, the landscape became ever more threatening, the settlements ever more inadequate to deal with the hostility of the vast barren space. Great stretches of drab fields were broken by towns which seemed to offer little hope against the immense brutal desolation that overpowered everything and rendered it meaningless. There was too much of it, too much empty space stretching in every direction to the straight horizon. The only difference between land and sky was a subtle shading of beige. The entire scene was one blank canvas. There's no place for people here, thought Jenny, gazing into the distance with senses dulled by monotony. This land negates human purpose. The people, the structures they put up, make no impression. This land destroys human identity."

"What's wrong with that?" I queried, a little breathless.

"Spare me. Everyone knows the prairie is a god-forsaken, barren, soulless monster who eats her young."

A gnarled petrified twig perched on the edge of a chair, Aunt Olive at eighty-four, was preserved by the smoke that spiraled from her nose and mouth on a more or less continuous basis. Her hair was still black, suspiciously without a hint of grey, her skin a smooth brown paste, her teeth incredibly white and even.

We were in my kitchen. I had suggested hers because of Gully, who had been demoted to a curtained corner in the living room, an arrangement much like that in Russian novels where several families share a flat. Lara and Rowlf had gone to the ranch for a few days. Lara wanted to introduce Rowlf to her father and brother, the sane members of the family, as she put it. I was happy to lend them my car, thinking of a blessed few days when I could get down to work. Not that they were physically intrusive, since they didn't emerge until noonish. What they did in their room all morning I didn't want to think about, even if it was legal. But at least they were now clean while doing it. And quiet. Their first day after settling in, rock guitar riffs had erupted through the walls. I'd had to inform Rowlf that the apartment was a writer's retreat with strict rules about silence. "Oh, you mean like in a monastery?" he said. "Cool. No sweat." He beamed me his quirky smile full of child wonder and after that the silence from that area was both deafening and somehow ominous, as though the little darlings were constructing a bomb.

On the domestic front things were trucking along, although it got a little dicey with the visiting nurse. I had to assume a mild heart condition exacerbated by my mountain experience that needed monitoring, nothing serious, only occasionally uncomfortable.

Back to Aunt Olive – she had informed me in a loud stage whisper over the phone that we *had* to meet at my place, she'd tell me all about it. I had to rely on personally supervising the placement of plugs in Gully's ears. "If at any time I don't hear something…" I left the threat unfinished.

"What if I have to think?" he said.

"Thought has never been an element in your work," I said. At that he looked hurt.

Then he recovered. "You're joking, aren't you? You always did have that wry sense of humour."

I closed the kitchen door – a wide sliding one – firmly behind me. I advised Aunt Olive to speak in low tones. Not that I expected either of us to be telling outrageous secrets, but I didn't want Gully to know so much as my grocery list.

"Why did you let the s.o.b. back in, anyway?" was her response. "After what he did to you? I woulda plugged him fulla holes."

"You can't just plug somebody full of holes."

"Why not?"

"It's illegal."

"Not if they don't catch you."

Hastily, I changed the topic to my typed pages.

"What you need is a different muse," was her advice. She flicked her ashes in the general direction of the ashtray. "This one's the pits."

I looked at her quickly. Her face was impassive, her blink without guile. I watched bits of ash float and descend into the coffee puddle. She couldn't possibly know about Harry and I did not want to tell her. I did not want to admit, even to Aunt Olive, that I had a man in my bed who pretended I wasn't there.

"What you need to do," she went on in her smoky voice, "is get out more. No wonder you write this kind of stuff. Stuck in your room all day with a machine that computes words. Get real. Kick up your heels. Join life. Join a club. Come with me to aerobics."

I looked across the table at those old eyes. She did not understand my obsession. How could she? Until seven years ago when I had moved into the building, we had seen each other mostly at organized events such as birthdays and holidays. During the last seven years my writing had been strictly business. She did not know that things had changed. She did not know that I had returned to all that I had happily left when I married my last husband. She did not know that I *had* to cocoon myself in my room with my computer. That was part of the job description. She did not know that only when I was living in an imagined world could I be sure of my existence in what people imagined to be the real one. I opened my mouth to say some of this to her but then closed it. What was the use of trying to make anyone who is not a writer understand?

In truth, it did seem unreal even to me. Weeks of my life boiled down to a few pages in the lives of my characters, weeks during which I had sweated blood without any help from Harry. Even the wink, I realized later, had come not from him but from the wishful imaginings of my mind, and when I read over the words I had written since taking to our mutual bed, they seemed ill-conceived.

Still, I was determined. If Gully could do it, so could I. I had set myself up a schedule and tried to adhere to it. I forced myself to type words that would appear on the screen... '... that was all she could remember, the snow lying deep and the thermometer attached to the outside of the frosted window registering forty below in the early morning.'

I flipped through a few pages and read from another scene. "This is several years later," I explained. "'Jenny lay huddled beneath the blankets with her babies. In a moment, John would get up to start the fire. Through the small window, she could see the only light, glittering stars against the black. She could feel the utter stillness and utter cold. Beside her, John stirred, rolled over, stuck an arm out into the icy air of the room and lit a match.'"

In the margin, I had penned in a note: metaphor, long winter night of the soul, time spent in room with Harry, spinning story. The darkest hour, before the lighting of the fire.

"What happens next?" Aunt Olive broke into my concentration.

"John gets up and gets the fire going and goes out to feed the livestock and Jenny gets up and makes breakfast. The chapter ends with him looking up at the stars."

"But what happens?"

"He's outside looking at the stars, see. Like, he's living his dream, which is free land, building an empire, all that. But what about her dreams? She's stuck inside and can't see the stars. She can't see anything but drudgery and sick kids and toil."

"And then what?"

"What?"

"What happens?"

"Nothing."

"Something has to happen."

"It's a realistic depiction of life in a homesteader's shack."

"Real life is dull. Real people lead dull ordinary lives. You have to spice it up. Something must happen. Doesn't one of the babies die or something?"

"I hadn't planned on it."

"Okay. What happens in the next scene?"

"Jenny bakes bread. It's bread making day."

"And then..."

"She melts snow water to wash clothes."

"That sounds interesting."

"I'm putting in details of the farm woman's lot in life. Details are interesting. Haley did very well with details. So did Michener."

"He wrote about interesting places like Hawaii. And he spiced it up. Say, I've got an idea. What if this tall dark handsome fellow knocks on the door, and John hires him, and Jenny falls in love with him, and they get it on, you know, and Jenny gets pregnant, but she doesn't tell John that it might not be his, so she has the baby, and the hired hand leaves and she's heartbroken but years later he returns..."

"Hold it!" I put up both hands as if fending off a physical attack. I looked sharply at Aunt Olive. How did she know the story of my life? But her face was bland of any underlying meaning. She had pulled that plot line out of a typical romance novel. The story was a cliché, my life was a cliché.

My quintessential prairie novel, on the other hand, had artistic integrity. It was based on Aunt Olive's life, loosely of course. "I want to be true to the vision," I pleaded for understanding. "To the characters, to you Aunt Olive. This is your story. I want to be true to you!"

"Don't be. I wanted lights, I wanted excitement."

"I can get that in. How your inner self longed for romance. How your creativity was thwarted, how you never had a chance to fulfill your dreams."

"Jesus Murphy girl, it wasn't that bad. Besides, that's not a plot. What's the action?"

"This is not supposed to be a plot driven story. The reader is supposed to get interested in the characters."

"So far I'm not interested. And if I'm not interested in my story, who else is gonna be?"

I blinked quickly several times. I felt cut to the quick. I had slaved in my room for days on end only to be told that my work was worthless. Aunt Olive must have seen my disappointment. Her face softened like a collapsed suede pouch. "Okay," she said, "let's start over. Tell me in one sentence what it's about?"

"What it was like to be a homesteader's wife in the early part of the century."

"And..."

"And what?"

"That's not a sentence." Have I mentioned that Aunt Olive, after she was finished with being a homesteader's wife, went to school and became an English teacher? "What about being a homesteader's wife?"

"It was a killer. Nothing but drudgery and disappointment."

"How about sex?"

"You can't have sex in a prairie novel."

"Why not?"

"I don't know. Prairie novels never have sex."

"They must've had sex. They sure as hell had lotsa kids."

"We just skip over that part."

Aunt Olive contemplated a moment. "Come to think about it, we didn't have much sex. Too bloody cold. But that doesn't mean you can't put it in the novel. And violence. How about if the tall dark handsome rogue of a stranger returns and tries to take up where he left off and John shoots him."

Now Aunt Olive was writing my story and getting it all wrong. The stranger did not return and life simply went on. I had another baby and started taking courses at the university. I signed up for Harry's course and he started coming to the ranch on weekends. My husband quite enjoyed his company. His amours, often close to Lara's age, would go off riding with the children in the morning, help me in the kitchen in the evening, and cry on my shoulder when it was over with Harry.

"It's not that kind of story." I said.

"Make it that kind of story."

"I don't have a model. I don't know any murderers."

"Maybe you do."

I looked deep into her old eyes. They were covered by a yellow gelatinous film. "What do you mean?"

"You never know about someone's past. In the old days, we settled our own grievances. Nobody knew what went on in the bush. We didn't need anyone from the outside who didn't know the circumstances telling us what to do."

I could only stare at the lines around her lips, pleating and unpleating like an accordion in motion.

"A lot of people have murder in their hearts," the pleats kept on. "Imagine them actually taking the big step. Make it up."

"You have to write about what you know."

"What I know is something has to happen. Else, you don't have a story."

"But nothing did happen. That's the reality. I want to remain true to the integrity of the documentation of a place and its people. I want to remain true to Uncle Owen." I clamped my lips. I had not meant to say that name. After twenty years, Aunt Olive still choked up at mention of her beloved.

Uncle Owen had been Aunt Olive's husband who had come back from the second world war with several medals and only one arm. A rugged survivor, a classic prairie homesteader of the Frederick Philip Grove variety, he had taken free DVA land in the Peace. As a little girl I'd been in love with Uncle Owen. Fascinated by the empty sleeve of his work shirt, I would stare at it for hours, imagining what it looked like. Shriveled and dangling? A bloody mess? A severed stump? Uncle Owen swore it itched in hot weather and ached in damp. I believed him. To me that absent arm was a living breathing entity. I have to say even now, the mystery and magic of his absent arm had determined my life, had made my affair with a ranch hand and the subsequent break up of my marriage inevitable.

"I can't degrade his memory by turning his story into a cheap melodrama. He had to be so tough to survive."

Aunt Olive looked at me with fierce eyes. "Put him in New York or better still L.A. Make him a police detective. He had the nature for it. Hey, I've got it. Make him a Dirty Harry type. That's how he lost his arm, in a shoot-out where he's saving the beautiful victim from someone who has taken her hostage."

"I suppose I could have him lose it in an auger." I said. "Lots of men lost arms in augers."

"Forget it." She lit another cigarette from the one burned down to the tips of her fingers. "No respectable romantic hero is gonna lose his arm in an auger, I don't care what you say. You got any more coffee there?"

I stood up. "If I make him a police detective, I'm betraying my character."

"Your uncle Owen would have saved the victim, if he'd been there."

"I'm writing serious stuff, original material about real people with real problems, culminating in some great philosophical revelation." I poured us both another coffee and returned the carafe to the hot plate. "Don't you see?" I pleaded, desperate to make her understand, since I was using her experiences as a model. "I want to write about this land that broke people's hearts. I want to write about what really happened on the prairie. I truly believe that this material is worth documenting for history, for future generations, so young people will know what it was like. This is important, meaningful work, and prairie writers have a responsibility to tackle it. People lost their crops year after year to hail or drought or frost or blight. People were beaten down by life, destroyed by the elements, by isolation and loneliness, by years, decades, of getting up before daylight and having to light a fire in thirty-below weather and what if they couldn't get a fire going!"

"Hey, calm down." She jerked her head and her thumb toward the living room, reminding me.

I lowered my voice to a whisper. "I can't help it. I put myself in their place, nothing but dog work all day, sick children and no doctors. How many children died or were deformed or retarded because there were no doctors or hospitals? Those poor women! Someone needs to write their story. No light. Can you imagine what it was like when it got dark at four-thirty in the afternoon and you knew there would be no light until eight-thirty the next morning and you didn't have electricity or an unlimited supply of coal oil or kerosene or whatever the hell they used then. Can you *imagine*!"

"I don't have to imagine," she said. "I lived it."

"I want to write about a mother's heart being broken," I said softly.

"Every day in this city a mother's heart is being broken. Who cares?"

Her voice turned wobbly which indicated she may not be as tough as she seemed. "I'm glad you have Fred," I said.

"Don't mention that name to me." The wobble snapped tight and turned brittle as a twig in winter. "That son-of-a-bitch."

I was flabbergasted.

"That's why we couldn't have coffee at my place," she said. "He's there doing his laundry."

"What happened?"

"His machine broke down."

"I mean, why are you mad at him?

"The old fool." Her voice was positively venomous. "Some young thing bats her eyelashes at him and he becomes stupid. She's in the same aerobics class. They shouldn't open those classes to the public."

I was going to remind her that Fred, who lived in a high rise around the corner, would then not be eligible to attend, but she didn't leave an opening. "Oh, it's not the first time. There was that woman in the elevator."

"What woman?"

"You know. I told you about her."

I remembered her going on about Fred being ga-ga over some woman he had met in the elevator but I hadn't paid attention to the details. She was always imagining something of the sort. I had always thought it was kind of cute, the way she persisted in thinking all young women were after Fred and that at seventy-three he would have the energy to care. But it suddenly struck me that maybe it wasn't cute. "You mean the one who was murdered?" A chill entered my veins.

"That's the one. Probably messed around with some other woman's man. Probably deserved it."

"Aunt Olive!" But, no, the idea that had entered my mind was entirely too preposterous. I couldn't bear it if Aunt Olive was the murderer.

"If thine eye offend thee, pluck it out," she went on. "That's the bible."

"That's not…"

"If you'd got rid of Gully years ago, he wouldn't be bothering you now."

"You can't just get rid of people."

"Why not, when they do you dirt like he did you? Instead, you let him suck you in again."

"He didn't have any place else to go," I said. "He's getting old. I think he's reformed."

"A leopard doesn't change his spots."

"Maybe I was a little lonely." I startled myself with the words, but once they were out I knew they were true. "That was before Lara came back."

"Some people will do crazy things to try and get around loneliness, but in the end you can't go around it. You have to set your jaw and go straight through."

I looked at her and wondered. "How do you get through?"

She thought a moment. "Don't try and stop the pain. Let it flow in and out." She placed her hands on her knees and pushed herself up off the chair. She took a moment to arrange her joints satisfactorily. "Remember," she said. "No more of that prairie shit."

"Yeah."

"Get out of that room. Live a little. How about that Sergeant Rock?"

"What about him?"

"He's perfect."

"Get real. Anyway, he's probably married."

"Not any more. She left him when he lost his arm."

"How do you know that?"

"I asked him. I made him a coffee."

"Did he take off his hat?"

She frowned. "Come to think of it, he didn't."

As I slid open the kitchen door, I could hear Gully's steady rhythm. It continued as we made our way to the hall door where Aunt Olive turned. "If all else fails," she whispered, "let Jenny have an accident. Put her out of her misery."

I looked at the floor. I could feel her black eyes on me. "Don't worry," I whispered back. "Something is going to happen."

"What?"

"Something." I opened the door.

She took a step. "Come to aerobics in the morning," she said in a normal voice. "No, don't say no. If you're not there, I'll come up here and haul you down. I want a second opinion on that floozy." She stopped in the middle of the doorway and looked back. "Sex," she said in a false whisper that shouted in my ears. "Sex is life and life is sex. Put in more sex. That gets them every time."

As I closed the door, I saw a blur of something rounding a corner. Rock. The sight had become familiar – the flick of a grey coattail, the heel of a well-shod copper's shoe, in the halls, in the foyer, disappearing through a door. He could move quickly for such a solidly constructed individual.

I stared at the closed door. The picture in my mind wasn't grey, wasn't solid. When I narrowed my eyes and thought harder, I didn't see a well-shod copper's shoe. I saw a slim ankle in an ankle strap attached to an extremely high red heel.

7.

─❦─

AS I TURNED BACK INTO THE ROOM, I could feel my forehead
forming its famous furrow. What was that red shoe doing
on the twelfth floor? Then I forgot about the shoe because I was
struck with the barrage of Gully's tapping from the other side
of his curtain. It sounded like a rock band drummer on speed,
the beats tripping over themselves in wild excitement. Was he
faking it? Was he pretending to be engaged in his work when
in reality he had been eavesdropping on my conversation with
Aunt Olive? I raised my foot to march in on him and demand
an explanation when, behind me, there was a knock. Thinking
Aunt Olive had forgotten something, I flung wide the door.
When I saw who it was, I closed it just as quickly, only to have
it stopped by a copper's laced oxford, then nudged open by a
substantial grey shoulder. Rock was in.

"Yes?" I could feel the furrow becoming a major excavation.
I could hear the annoyance in my voice. Was I never to get any
writing done this day?

"I wonder if I might have a word with you." He didn't bother
trying for a pleasant expression. What he did was raise his
head toward the kitchen, much like my sad-eyed dog used to
do when scenting a rib bone. In this case it was the coffee I'd
brewed for Aunt Olive.

"Would you like a coffee?" Where had the words come
from? I could scarcely admit they were mine. Was it Aunt
Olive's influence?

"Don't mind if I do." His words were equally surprising. He was not the cozy chat over coffee type. His next words were downright alarming, "How's the star boarder?" My mind flew about like a bird out of its cage. Then I realized, he meant Harry. He knew nothing of Gully, who was disturbingly quiet behind his curtain, unable to make a sound for fear of being detected, thus able to hear everything we said.

"Shhh," I hissed, picturing Gully's ears as huge radio receivers, hoping that, if he had heard, he would construe the star boarder as Lara. Quickly, I herded Rock along, out of the danger zone and into the kitchen. I snapped the door tightly behind us, but not before I heard Gully once more take up his frantic activity. I made as much noise as I could – rattling the coffee maker, the cups, the saucers which we didn't need with mugs, slammed the fridge door repeatedly and kept up a steady inane chatter.

Seated and spooning sugar into his coffee, Rock, still in hat and coat – he declined my offer to remove same – told me the reason for his visit. "We're closing the case."

I watched his right hand spoon another two spoons of sugar and tried not to look at his left arm. "You've found the murderer?"

"No. We don't have anything to go on. No body, no DNA, no fingerprints, other than hers of course, but nothing to match them to. No leads. All we have is an anonymous phone call, a smear of blood, a man's footprint in that blood and blood on a knife. We have no matches on the blood. We've done all the lab work, run all the forensics, tracked all the clues. We've run a few hundred computer profiles and have come up with nothing. The particulars on her application form for the apartment were false, which throws a suspicious light on her activities, but we haven't been able to find out what they were. Could be she was hiding from someone. A husband, maybe. Husbands and wives run away and hide from each other more often than you'd think. Could be she was involved in illegal activity. Often people involved in drug trafficking or terrorism rent or buy a place for a few months under false names while they put their plans into operation. We've given what we've got to Interpol. Because of the G-8 Summit."

"G-8?"

"At Banff. You know, the meeting of all those bigwigs."

"Oh." I had been so busy not writing, I hadn't kept up with the news.

"A case is never entirely closed until we solve it but for now my superior needs me on something else." Those blue eyes were steady on me. "The fact is, some people do get away with murder."

His words made me think of Aunt Olive's words. But another thought struck me. "So my hus ... former husband is in the clear?"

"He's been in the clear for some time. We scrapped the mistaken identity idea. It appears that you were never in danger. I've been trying to contact you. You don't answer my messages." His look was severe, penetrating.

My eyes fell from the accusation in his. They lighted on that empty sleeve, so neatly pressed, so neatly folded into his pocket. The mystery of that sleeve, the presence of the arm that had once inhabited that sleeve sent shivers up my spine.

"That's it then." He stood. "And the patient?" It seemed like an afterthought.

"Still comatose, I'm afraid." I whispered. "He's very sensitive to noise."

"I'm sure Missing Persons is keeping track of his progress."

"Yes."

He opened the kitchen door. Gully's tapping ceased abruptly but not soon enough. "You have someone here?"

"My daughter."

"I see ... well, then ... thanks for the coffee."

At the door, I had a thought. "You wouldn't happen to know...?"

"Yes?"

I was about to ask about the woman in red shoes. Just in time I remembered Gully. I didn't want him to know about the woman. I didn't want him to know my business.

"Nothing." I closed the door on Rock and stood a moment, my back against it. His inquiry about Harry had seemed like an afterthought. It struck me. Rock would not have an afterthought. He was too well organized to have an afterthought.

Gully had started again and was already into his rhythm. I looked toward his curtain. It was a thick curtain of heavy material with a spiral of smoke rising above. Except for the hacking cough coming from behind, he might have been the genie in the lamp. I'd spent two whole day at Sears, the Bay, Zeller's, Wal-Mart, scouting out the heaviest cheap drapes I could find. The tapping coming from behind that curtain spelled focus. Keep your eye on your work, he said to me once. It might have been when I was bringing him snacks to sustain him while he was stealing my novel. If you have anything else on your mind, he said, you're going to screw up.

A month before, I wouldn't have believed it, that he could reinvent himself from that burned-out bum into a productive human being. Showered and shaved, wearing clean shirt and jeans, except for being still painfully thin, he looked much like the Gully of the newspaper stories. But why was I surprised? Gully had always been a hard worker and ambitious. He was applying to himself his words about inspiration and perspiration.

A greater surprise was his reaction to the news that he had a daughter. He didn't so much as raise his eyebrows. I surmised that likely he had several children floating around the globe, some of whom he knew about, some of whom he didn't.

The very day Lara and Rowlf arrived, I knew I had to get the revelation over with. Gully would guess the truth because of Lara's age and because, quite frankly, she looked like him. Lara would know the truth because I had shared those newspaper stories with her. Lara provided me with an opening. Directly after moving herself and Rowlf into the spare room, she bombed into the kitchen, threw open the fridge, banged a few cupboard doors and announced in outraged derogation, "There's nothing to eat around here!" With grave misgivings and multiple dire warnings, all met with her sneer, I gave her my credit card and sent the little darlings out for supplies. I then summoned Gully. I informed him that we would have to alter living arrangements and the person he was altering them for was his daughter. I warned him to be kind if he didn't want to find himself out on the street.

Lara had the advantage of knowing that she had a father. From her infancy, I had tried to be forthcoming about him, making up plausible excuses for why we were not together, even showing her newspaper clippings of his presence at writer's festivals and such. She talked about meeting him, yet didn't want me to make a move in that direction. I didn't push the issue. I assumed he wouldn't want to meet her and I didn't want her to get hurt. Perhaps she, too, was afraid of rejection. But when I told her that the man who was vacating the extra bedroom and taking up abode in a corner of the living room was her father, she was hysterical with delight. Like a little kid, she jumped up and down and clapped her hands with glee. "Does this mean you're getting back together?" she trilled.

"No." My voice was emphatic.

That very evening, I took the occasion of a communal dinner, which I prepared, to introduce them formally. I told Gully that he had to attend, as it turned out, an unnecessary demand. He opened his arms and she walked into them. After that, she was like a little puppy, dancing around him, bringing him coffee, wondering what she could do to be of assistance to him. Conversely, at other times, she became exaggeratedly quiet, tiptoeing around the apartment in a manner that was disquieting. Amazingly, he, who would never tolerate interference with his writing, seemed to get a kick out of her. He must have observed the resemblance. Maybe he viewed her as an extension of himself whom he adored. Still, I expected a blow-up on his part. I cautioned her: "He never speaks when he's writing. He doesn't want to lose anything to life that should be put down on the page."

"Do you think I don't know what artists are like?" she scorned. "Half of the people in our commune were artists."

As to the logistics of our communal living, I decided to handle the situation as though we were marooned on a desert island and had to get along to survive. Rowlf wholeheartedly adopted the idea and volunteered to prepare dinners. At first I thought, no way, José. I wouldn't be able to swallow a mouthful even if he was now presentably clean and clothed. There was still the issue of body piercings and hair that must have taken hours to sculpt and of which I could detect no change since its arrival. I thought of eighteenth-century England, the high elaborate hairstyles, the cootie bags women wore around their necks. Besides, I didn't want a stranger in my kitchen and, to top things off, I did not relish dinner companions, especially in the form of my ex husband. But then I realized that one dinner together was more efficient and less disturbing than each party making noise in the kitchen at various times. And the plan would give me extra writing, or non-writing, time. As it turned out, the meals were surprisingly tasty. Also, as it turned out, Gully didn't attend them. Lost in the labyrinth of his novel, he scarcely came up for air. About midnight, blind with exhaustion, he would stumble to the kitchen, grab leftovers or bread and cheese, then fall into a deep, short sleep before making himself a huge pot of coffee and going at it again in early morning.

My back still against the door, I considered Rock. He *was* attractive in a cop sort of way. But how could I ever be sure it was him and not his absent arm I was after?

Gully's drumming disturbed my thoughts. He must have gotten some fresh ideas. Which was what I desperately needed. In fact, our production seemed to be in inverse proportion – the more fast and furious his, the more slow and lethargic mine. I shuffled into my room, throwing the dead bolt behind me. Today would be another day that I would not get a message from Harry. No wonder Aunt Olive pronounced my prairie document uninspired, pedantic, in short, boring. I cursed the thing in me that wouldn't let me quit. Why couldn't I be like Aunt Olive, get myself a boyfriend, go to exercise class, take up a hobby, watch television?

Resigned to my fate, I stood over Harry. I studied him. No change, it seemed. And yet something was different. The notes between him and the edge of the bed, to which had been added some source material, seemed to have shifted. The piles were not quite as squared off. Had Harry moved? Had he moved and I'd missed it? I felt frantic. To quell my heart, I lay down beside him. I lay there a long while, stiff and unmoving, waiting for him to move again, waiting for him to speak to me, waiting for the sound of my grandfather's voice. All I heard was silence. I got up and sat down at my blank screen. Sometimes my last words of a session spurred me into making the leap into the current session. I clicked words onto the screen. I read my last sentence. "That's it for now, I need to pee."

An article in *Writer's Digest* about writer's block said to put down a word, any word, then that word will logically be followed by another. I started typing ... today I don't need to pee, some days I need to pee and some days I don't. Guess it depends on how much water I drink, or don't drink, or how much wine I drink or don't drink, or how much beer I drink or don't drink. I suddenly stopped. This was going nowhere. I doubted that I would ever find a place in my writing to fit in my pee. The idea behind free writing was that you would eventually use the collected raw material. When you need this *lumber* to build your house, there it will be, in your basement in one of those brown cardboard boxes piled behind the furnace. Yes, boys and girls. Some day when you are writing away on your novel, you'll think, aha, I wrote some stuff on that ten years ago. The big challenge will be to find it. But even if you can't, trekking off to the storeroom allows multi hours to be spent doing something important and necessary for your writing that is not writing. One drawback – if you do locate the pages you have in mind, if you do emerge hours later from the dust, triumphant, with a tattered box of old writing and read again those unbelievable insights and striking images, you may find that you can't use the material after all, that it will not lend itself to what you are now writing or ever will write and, besides, it was bad writing in the first place. You close the file like skin over a wobble fly nest.

I stared at the screen and tried to conjure up a picture of Jenny, but instead of the homestead shack I saw a red high-heeled shoe disappearing around a corner in a hallway, an image I found immensely disturbing. Why? I asked myself. I was not the only resident on the twelfth floor. Obviously, the shoe did not belong to the retired university professor or the elderly woman with a walker, but it could very well belong to a visitor of one of them. Somehow, I didn't think so. In all the years of my residency, there had never been a red shoe like that on this floor – such a brilliant red, the heel about four inches, the ankle strap so small, to fit only the most delicate ankle. And there had been something about the movement, quick, even furtive. The person wearing that shoe did not want to be seen. The mystery of the red shoe on the twelfth floor. I said it out loud. I rather liked the sound of it.

Stop it! I interrupted my fascination with a stern admonishment. You are writing the quintessential prairie novel not fabricating nonsense about a red shoe.

But when I closed my mind to the red shoe, I also closed it to Jenny. Nothing surfaced. Your passionate nature needs to be fulfilled. The words seemed like a mantra that, if repeated often enough, would be the *open sesame* to all lost narratives. But magic was unavailable at the moment. My fingers had been poised over the keyboard for so long they were becoming fossils. In an attempt to reactivate them, I stretched them wide. I clenched and unclenched my fists. I looked at the letters of the alphabet beneath the claws of my hands, letters that I had to form into words and then the words into sentences and then the sentences into two or three hundred pages that made sense. It was too much. I felt utterly defeated by the sheer weight of letters.

I glanced toward the window. I couldn't remember when we had had so much snow. I fully expected it to rise to the windowsill of my twelfth floor apartment. I felt that I was a prisoner in a glass snow globe of whirling flakes. And I had been in it, excepting the two coffee breaks, since four a.m. when, frustrated at not being able to toss and turn for fear of disturbing Harry, I had given up and rolled out of my side of the bed.

The fact was, I could not come up with anything, worthwhile or not, after Aunt Olive's and Rock's visits. Maybe my prairie material was uninspired, but at least I was able to get some words onto the screen. Now, thanks to being knee-capped by my dear aunt and bushwhacked by Rock, I couldn't even write dull boring stuff.

I grabbed a jacket from the closet and, careful to lock both locks on my bedroom door behind me, tiptoed past the click-ety-click of Gully's keys and on out into the hall. There, I found my octogenarian neighbour in a befuddled state looking for her lost cat, which allowed me an hour of aimless wandering through corridors and out onto the street. Large flakes of snow were drifting down. It wasn't cold. Since the day was shot anyway, I decided to go for a walk along the river.

Striding along, I drew deep draughts of fresh air into my lungs, deep into my belly. I let it out from my belly and drew more in. It felt so good to breathe. Aunt Olive was right. I needed to get out more. I passed by the market, by the fountain stilled by winter, and crossed over the footbridge leading into the park. Below me, the lagoon was white and frozen. Before me, a young couple with long legs in skin-tight jeans walked with their arms around each other. They stopped on the side of the bridge to kiss. As I passed, their bodies were pressed into each other. She was whispering into his ear.

It hit me.

Harry was not the sort of man to speak first. He suffered from the same sickness as I, the fear of getting to know anyone really well, the fear of emotional burdens. How many times had I seen Harry make a move on a woman then draw back? Maybe it was an instinctual reaction, a crab at the bottom of the ocean reaching out a claw and recoiling it back when it touched something. Or maybe he questioned himself – do I want to become involved? The answer was always no, as it was with me. Neither of us wanted a relationship that would demand too much of ourselves. Neither of us wanted to have to be the way another person wanted us to be. Neither of us wanted a real person in a real relationship. We did not want to be disappointed. We did not want to lose the dream. We were afraid we couldn't keep it going. And, finally, neither of us wanted to lose our solitude. It was a congenital ailment, having to do with the sky under which we were born, a prairie sky. We learn to be alone. We like it. Solitude is our comfort zone.

I turned quickly and retraced my steps. I zipped through the front door, up the elevator, into my apartment. I took out my jangle of keys and unlocked my bedroom door, but it was already unlocked. I was sure I'd locked it. I distinctly recalled locking it. I glanced toward Gully's corner. His typing had the sound of focused concentration that had been going on for a while. Besides, he didn't have a key. Lara and Rowlf didn't have a key. No one except me had a key to this door. I must have forgotten to lock it. The strain of the last few weeks was getting to me, to my memory to be exact. I was losing it. No one could unlock that door from the outside. I caught my breath. Harry. Was Harry holding out on me?

I stood beside the bed and studied Harry. He seemed to be exactly where I had left him, in the exact same position, on his back, hands folded across his front. I looked at his ears, big, untidy ears, the openings large and shadowy. I had never before noticed his ears. Thirty-six years, I thought, and I don't know much about the man. I don't know the inside of him. I don't know the pulsing of his heart, the absolute darkness of the private place of his body's cavity.

I looked down at the face of my youthful dreams and expectations. I made myself see the changed face, made my eyes probe the trenches of cheek and forehead. Saddening at the slightly bitter downturn of the mouth, I realized that I was going to have to take extreme measures. Otherwise, I'd be in this room forever. I must sort out the puzzle of Harry. I must discover a way to make him yield his innermost self to me. But first I had to solve the problem of bringing him back to life. The fundamentals of keeping him warm and nourished weren't going anywhere. I must imagine a different approach to get him to tell me the story of landscape I needed to know.

I put on my fuzzy pink pyjamas, even though it was still daylight. But Harry was always like an icicle. I could hear the whisper of my slippers on the carpet, the sigh of my pyjama legs as I rounded to my side of the bed. I lay down, straight on my back as always. Then I was beneath the covers. Then I was turned toward him. Then I had one arm across his midsection. Then I put one of my warm pink legs across his cold thighs. Then I coiled my body around his. Then I placed my lips to the shadowy spiral of his ear.

8.

—⊲⊗⊳—

T HE SCENE OPENED BEFORE MY EYES like a surrealistic canvas. Two substantial buttocks bobbing on either side of a
thin rope of thong directly in my line of vision caused me to
wince. Surrounding me was a roomful of like-garbed individuals
hopping up and down and waving arms to ear-splitting music.
On my left was an old guy in boxer shorts imprinted with palm
trees and a T-shirt emblazoned with flamingos. He was tall and
lean except for a slight beer belly that overhung the elastic of
his shorts, baggy at the back because of his shrunken bum.
But he still had good legs, strong and straight, he still had a
mane of thick lovely grey hair, he still was good looking if you
discounted sagging jowls and loose neck skin.

He was Aunt Olive's Fred. He wasn't jumping up and down
quite like the others but, then, neither was I. He was moving his
old joints in a careful fashion as best he could to the raucous
noise. "Step touch, one and two and three and four, knees
up, double it up, grape vine right, bring it back, circle it out,
centre it back," the cute little female instructor at the front of
the class might have been calling a square dance instead of a
fitness class.

Fred was slightly in front of me. I could see in the pitiless
fluorescent light that he was working up a sweat, when out of
nowhere came a whirling dervish. She was long and she was
tall. And did I mention young? Young with abundant dark
hair, wearing very brief shorts and a halter top, her gazelle

legs might have been on springs. To my utter astonishment, she hopped over to Fred and leaned very close into his ear and whispered something. Just the way she moved, just the way she whispered, I judged her words to be obscene. They both laughed. She contrived to rub her boobs against Fred's pink flamingos as she leaned into him. She looked over her shoulder, furtively I thought. Then she leaped to the water fountain and back to her spot at the front of the room where she could watch herself in the mirror.

I could see what Aunt Olive had been talking about.

It was seven a.m. and I was in the second-floor exercise room of our complex. Large windows overlooked a busy street below. In the distance, through the trees, was the river, a pleasant aspect in summer. In winter, everything was white, the trees stark pencil sticks against it. Suddenly my stomach felt queasy. I thought I might throw up right there in the middle of the gym. I brought myself down from medium intensity to low. I closed my eyes a moment. When I opened them, there in front of me was a character in search of an author.

She wore black tights and a pink sleeveless top with something filmy and transparent over it. The former revealed a surprising buttock construction, unusual in a woman with such skinny legs. The latter revealed jiggly arms and undefined bosoms. She was in full makeup, including false eyelashes, even at this hour of the morning. Her frizzy black hair was piled on top of her head, held there by a pink bow. It crossed my mind, against my will, that she resembled an ungroomed poodle. On her feet were black ballerina slippers – she was the only one in the class without sturdy joggers. It struck me as so surprising – Aunt Olive was one of the loves of my life and before today I had not known the intimate shape of her body. Before today I had not seen her in heavy makeup. She was usually restrained in that department, as befitting a former farm wife and school teacher. I watched as she manoeuvred herself into position between Fred and Ms. Pogo Stick, cannily blocking

Fred's view with that of her own cute little saddle bags.

"I was going to trip her if she tried that again," she said to me after class. "Don't think I wouldn't have either."

"What?" I replied, taking the cotton balls out of my ears.

"That hotsy totsy."

"She's just having a bit of fun," I responded. That that young woman would be interested in Fred in that way was unbelievable even if he was good-looking for his age.

"The old coot," said Aunt Olive. "Did you see the way he couldn't take his eyes off certain parts of her anatomy?"

"She has some pretty fantastic moves," I ventured, recalling her wiggling this and that in Fred's face and the expression on that face, like a bull struck between the eyes with the blunt side of an axe.

"Silly old pot-bellied Lothario," grumped Aunt Olive.

That my aunt still *cared,* that was the amazing thing; that was the frightening thing. Was there to be no end to the striving of the human heart? Was there to be no rest even near the end? Was there to be no retirement from desire?

After making sure that Fred made it safely to the men's change room, we took the elevator up, the back one. They did not allow sweaty people in the front one. We were silent, each involved in her own thoughts, Aunt Olive likely hatching a plan to do away with Ms. Pogo and me trying to think where I had seen her before. Perhaps she had been a student. I was constantly running into former students, madly scanning my brain for names and places while they conversed with enthusiastic familiarity.

"Want a coffee?" Aunt Olive asked when the elevator stopped at number ten. I was about to refuse, I wanted to get at my writing but, I reasoned, I'd agreed to exercise at such an ungodly hour to sleuth out the situation and give my opinion. Besides, she looked so down I decided to gloss over the next half hour of her life with some bad-mouthing of Ms. Pogo, which turned into over an hour.

By the time I turned the key in the lock of my apartment door it was nearly ten and everyone was up and waiting for me. The scene revolved before my eyes, a vivid collage of faces needing my attention. To my right, through the kitchen doorway, Gully looked up from an open fridge. My first thought was – he must be starving to interrupt his writing. My second thought, fleeting because of the distractions, was – he's come out of his corner a lot lately. Is it because of Lara or is it to spy?

Rowlf hovered in the background shadows. His hands were held outward as if he was carrying something bloody in them. I had the impression that he was approaching an altar with his life's sacrifice. The more dominant figure, however, was my daughter. Lara was smack dab in front of me, head-on. I felt suddenly tired. I'd been hoping for a shower and a lie-down with Harry before anything happened. I hadn't even taken off my tights, for Cripe's sake!

Words were issuing forth from my daughter's mouth. "Rowlf and I want to get married." Suddenly, I went deaf. I watched her lips moving rapidly and tightly, clipping off words, but I could not comprehend what she was saying.

"What? What? I can't hear." Unfortunately, as soon as I spoke, my ears cleared, much as they do on an airplane.

"You heard me perfectly well," Lara snapped. "You just pretend you don't. You always do that. You never listen."

I could have said, I do too listen and she'd say no you don't, you never do, you didn't listen when I tried to tell you blah blah blah and I'd say I would have listened if you had told me, and on it would go. I decided to cut it short. "I thought you *were* married."

"We are. But we want to do it properly. Like, in the church and all." She tossed her long hair, amazingly shiny now that it was free of grime.

Astounded, I looked at my child. "You haven't been to church in twelve years! I distinctly remember when you were sixteen. You looked me in the eye and said that you weren't going to church, that you no longer believed in that patriarchal, medieval bullshit and that I couldn't make you."

"You should have made me. You should have taken control. I was only sixteen."

The injustice of this statement filled me with incoherent rage. Make her, indeed! Had she completely forgotten that, at age sixteen, she was a totally out of control brat.

I caught myself in time. If I wasn't careful, she would reduce me to the shrieking shrew of a decade ago when, faced with these daily wranglings, I would quite simply lose it. You have grown since then, I reminded myself. You are now a mature adult verging on old age. Also, the realization was slowly arriving – my daughter was not, in the eyes of the church, married to Rowlf. Maybe some unlicensed self-appointed mystic nutso had performed the ceremony. Maybe she wasn't married at all. Yippee, I thought, determined that this should remain so.

"Why you would marry that human pin cushion in the first place is beyond my understanding," I said. "Now you want to compound your error? You must be insane."

"I knew you'd take that attitude. And then you wonder why I never came to see you. I've had to defend every decision I've ever made. You're pitiful. You always judge people by their appearances."

"That's not true."

"It is so."

"My objection to Rowlf as a husband for my daughter has to do with the fact that at thirty years of age he doesn't have a focus and has never been gainfully employed."

"That just shows how much you're completely out of what's happening in today's world. You're back in the dark ages when marriage was based on the master/slave concept. Marriage nowadays is between two people, *people*, get it? I do what I want to do with my life, Rowlf does what he wants to do with his life, and we share those two lives. It's not a political or financial arrangement."

"Well, then, my question to you is how you, *you*, my intelligent, educated, not-to-mention beautiful daughter can be interested in a man who hasn't got it together by age thirty?" It must be great sex, I thought, but kept my mouth shut. I definitely didn't want to get into *that* discussion.

"I'll have you know that Rowlf has it very much together. He's a student."

"Ummm, I see. When is he going to get a degree?"

"He has three degrees. One is a Master's in sociology."

That took me back a bit but I wasn't about to admit it. "That's nice dear but why doesn't he *do* something with it? Couldn't he get a job teaching?"

"He's into research."

"Oh? What's he researching?"

"People. He's travelling across the country talking to people."

"But what's the topic. The focus."

"Just seeing how people live, what they're like and all."

"Is he writing a paper? And is this research to be published? Is it *serious*?"

"He's taking notes. He has a lot of notes." She paused. "He's got some pretty heavy decisions ahead of him."

"Oh?"

"He's making up his mind."

"Yes...?"

"Whether or not to do further graduate studies."

"Well, if he wants to teach at a university, or even go into the field... "

"The thing is ... he's thinking of changing direction, changing careers... Actually," she took a deep breath. "He's thinking of being a writer."

"Ahhh ... well, then, perhaps he doesn't really need a Ph.D. in sociology."

Rowlf's head was moving between Lara and me as if he were watching a ping pong match at which he was an objective observer. I suddenly realized that we were rudely having a conversation about him in front of him.

I turned back to Lara and caught, "now don't go ballistic..."

"I never go ballistic."

"You always go ballistic."

"That's the family myth. I no longer go ballistic."

"That's true. Don't get sarcastic."

"Why? What are you going to tell me?"

"Well, I was wondering, Rowlf was wondering, we both were wondering, if you'd sort of take him under your wing, y'know, sort of show him the ropes, about being a writer, I mean."

So far, Lara and I had not moved. We were still standing near the door, the tension in both our bodies holding us in place as though we were two figures at opposite ends of pulled elastic.

Well ... I ... uh ... I don't think ... Look ... I'm probably not the best person ... my books have been poetry ... how about your father?" Desperately, I glanced around for Gully but he had disappeared, slunk away as he always had in the face of responsibility.

"You used to teach creative writing. And you did freelance for years. Besides, you know as well as I do that Daddy is involved in an important project. His time is valuable... "

Daddy! Since when had Gully become Daddy?

"You can't expect him to interrupt... "

"Please... " I held out my hands in supplication to some god whose sense of humour was inappropriate.

Mistaking my gesture, Rowlf stepped forward from where he had been hovering. I noticed then that what he was holding was a manuscript, a large manuscript, which he placed in my numb outstretched hands.

'Twilight lay like a bloody smear on the sand. It was quiet, too quiet. The shore line, the shanty houses like stacked boxes, were dense with ominous stillness, while a thousand miles out in the ocean, the storm was already whipping itself into a frenzy, the wind gathering force, snarling in pain, frothing the waves. The ocean foaming at the mouth, swept onto the land like barbarian hordes, sniping its way across the shore, the beach, the beachfront hovels. It lunged toward the cringing town. And over it all, the wind howled in agony like a demonic voice of the sea, curdling out from the raw throat of the demonic beast of the storm that lay in wait for frail human beings who dared confront its rage.'

It was evening. Deciding that I might as well get it over with, I'd spent the afternoon skimming Rowlf's manuscript.

'Twilight gouged through the trees like fingers dripping blood. These last survivors, driven back to the north woods, the last place on earth where they might find refuge, huddled around the campfire. Brad knew that they were backed into a corner, that they would have to make a stand. He looked around at the little group, a band of misfits if ever there was one. Desiree sat directly across the clearing from him, the wild mane of her blonde hair swinging freely around her shoulders, the soft curves of her incredible body calling to him. That would have to wait, too. Now he had a job to do.

'As the sun descended below the horizon, the shadows lengthened. Dusk lay on the land like a funeral shroud. A sense of impending doom pervaded the air. Suddenly, Brad saw something where there had been nothing a few moments before, something like the black bare trunk of a tree. His eyes followed it up, up, up, until they were stopped by a black hard-shelled mass shutting out the sky.'

"I was thinking," Rowlf said. Perspiration beaded his brow. "Maybe describing twilight twice like that is too much."

"That's a thought."

"Although one is at the beginning of the novel and one is at the end. And then I was wondering if demonic isn't quite right there."

"Where?"

"Demonic beast. Maybe I should put ferocious."

"You *do* have demonic twice."

We sat in silence. We were at the kitchen table. I pretended to be reading the two paragraphs again. I was stalling for time so that I could think of something to say that would not be unkind. And I needed to be sure my reaction was not a jealous response to Rowlf's profuse production.

"Tell me," I said. "Have you written all this," I flipped through the pages, "since you've been here?"

"Mmmm. I can go like a crazy man when the muse hits."

I looked up quickly.

"The words just fall from my fingers like manna from heaven. Same with writing songs. I used to rip off half a dozen at a time, sometimes."

I regarded Rowlf's spiked burgundy and green hair, the earrings skirting his ear lobe and his guileless eyes. I tried to read the story in the design of his arms, thinking that there I might get a clue to his person. Unfortunately, the text was in a language foreign to me.

"One small point that you might want to consider..."

"Yes." His eagerness, his *hope*, was heartbreaking.

"If the storm is a beast attacking the land, then it's not exactly lying in wait."

Rowlf snapped his fingers. "Right on. Why didn't I see that? It's so obvious." He grabbed the pages from my hand and quickly scribbled out 'lay in wait' and in its place wrote 'demolished'. He looked across at me, pencil between his teeth.

"Or do you think 'totalled' would be more effective? Or ... I've got it!"

Quickly he scribbled out 'demolished' and wrote 'exterminated'. He handed the pages back to me, at the same time bestowing on me the self-satisfied look of an infant presenting his feces to his parent. "See, 'exterminated' goes with the whole theme of the beetles."

"I'm glad you brought that up, Rowlf," I said in my instructor voice. "I mean, theme. The beetles aren't the theme."

"They're not?" He frowned.

"No, they're the vehicle that carries your story. They're part of the plot." A cloud passed over the sunshine of Rowlf's face. "Let me ask you this, Rowlf," I said, in an attempt to clear it. "Let's just pose the question ... what would you say *is* the theme of your novel? Sometimes it helps if we know what we're trying to say."

"Theme?" Distress screwed his face.

"What is it about?" I had the grace to blush when I remembered that Aunt Olive had asked me the very same question only a couple of days before. "In the larger sense. I mean, I know it's about blood-sucking giant long-horned beetles who have gone berserk because of a radiation spill during a hurricane which causes them to grow to enormous proportions and have enormous appetites and they have this thirst for human blood, so we've got a disaster here, and these two experts, one an etymologist specializing in beetles and the other a sort of troubleshooter who goes all over the world solving disasters, have to try and figure out a way to stop them but nothing works, they're unstoppable, they're immune to any kind of chemical, which you very cleverly point out, is mankind's own fault because he has overused and abused chemicals and the environment so thoroughly in the past, now nothing works on these beetles." I took a deep breath. "That's the plot. But what is the theme."

"Hmmm. I'll have to think about that one." His brow creased.

Apparently, having to think made him hungry. He got up and went to the fridge. It had been two hours since dinner at six, the time agreed on for our communal meal. By seven we were all to be quiet, either back in our rooms or out. That may sound harsh, but the point was, those of us who wished to toil in the evenings could do so undisturbed. Gully had no problem with these arrangements. If he deigned to come out of his lair, he would eat quickly and promptly return to his window corner, to the laptop on a fold-up table. He was there now, contentedly tapping away until such time as he would lie down on his cot for the night. As for Lara, she had discreetly retired to her room.

"It seems to me, and please correct me if I'm wrong, but it seems to me that you want to say something about sowing the wind and reaping the whirlwind," I tried to coach Rowlf. He turned from where he was leaning into the fridge. His face was dark with puzzlement. Suddenly, it brightened. "I needed a way to have these beetles grow to gigantic proportions, see, so I thought, radiation, so then I needed a way to have those containers damaged and I had just seen that movie *A Perfect Storm* and I came up with this hurricane, so then I could have this long-horned beetle crawl through that radiation waste and then grow to gigantic proportions."

"But the hurricane also shows how nature can go on the rampage. What I mean is, in a general sense, you're trying to say that because we've abused the planet and nature that nature is taking revenge."

Rowlf smiled a sweet smile. "Exactly." He returned to the table with salami and bread laden with mayo, mustard, ketchup and relish, and proceeded to slap it all together. "That's why I have that first chilling chapter where that guy is taking his kids to that museum and there's that moth-eaten elk's head and that stuffed and mounted long-horned beetle, one and half inches long with antlers. That actually happened to me, by the way, when I was a kid, we were camping and my dad took us kids to this dusty old museum, and that's what they had on display. That kind of stuck in my head like. I mean, it was so bizarre, a stuffed long-horned beetle."

As Rowlf talked, I watched his mouth in fascination. Up until now I had tried not to look at it because of the tongue stud. He took a bite of his sandwich and chewed and continued telling me about how he and his folks were camping in the rain, which surprised me, oh not about camping in the rain since it always rains when one is camping, but the fact that Rowlf had been born into a family and not spawned in a hatchery. He told me how they had gone into this old museum to get out of the rain and how it had smelled of cold mould. I didn't hear his exact words. I was hypnotized by the mixture of half-chewed bread and salami and the stud revolving around in the mess.

"…don't you think?"

"Ummm…," I hedged, not having the faintest notion what he had been saying. "Let me ask you Rowlf … obviously you're writing a scifi horror combo…"

"Exactly. You got it." He seemed pleased.

"So, who are you reading these days? Like, which science fiction authors? There are so many good writers in that genre now. How about Stephen King?"

He shook his head vigorously in a negative motion. "Ummm," he chewed and swallowed. He took another bite. "That's one of my rules … never read when you're writing … otherwise you end up derivative. I don't want to be influenced by some-body else's writing."

"That might not necessarily be a bad thing," I looked up and down quickly.

"I want to be innovative."

"I'm not suggesting that you write exactly as they write or that you adjust your own particular voice … just that you might learn what the genre demands in terms of form."

"Nah." He shook his head so vigorously, a speck of mustard that had been deposited at the edge of his mouth flung sideways and hit the fridge.

"It's no different in a way than discussing your work at a writer's group."

"I'd never go to one of them," said Rowlf. "Have some insensitive, unknowledgeable dickhead tell me how to write my book? No way!"

"Okay… " I was reaching. "How about literary events," I suggested. "Have you ever gone to a literary reading?"

"What's a literary reading?" he asked in all innocence.

I sat back in my chair. I looked down at my hands in my

lap. I hadn't realized that I had folded them in an attitude of prayer, a prayer that had been answered. Suddenly I felt fine. I knew how I could convince Rowlf that he did not want to be a writer.

9.

———⊗⊗⊗———

"YOUR DAUGHTER IS A WONDERFUL PERSON."
I rummaged about in my mind. Who was Rowlf speaking about? I only had one daughter.

"She saved my life. Did she, like, tell you?"

"No ... I don't think so." I tried to remember if she might have, during one of those interminably long and boring discussions, which she favoured and which I abhorred.

Rowlf and I were driving along 17th Avenue on our way to the much-anticipated reading at the Night Gallery. I was busy praying that my old beater wouldn't quit suddenly, the way it had a habit of doing – a mechanic explained to me that it was air pockets in the gas line. It was not the sort of night you want to be stranded at the side of the road with the person your daughter sleeps with.

"It was down in L.A. I'd gone down there, see, with some people I met at a party in Vancouver. I was in this band and I met this guy at this party and he says whyn't you come with us down to L.A.? And I thought, hey why not, this might just be the chance of a lifetime, so I went to L.A. to write and record an album. After five months of rapping away at the industry's door I was starving and your daughter found me on the street and asked me would I like to help her cook at this church camp and, like, what was that like to a guy who's starving, you can imagine, she didn't have to ask twice. It was lonely down there, y'know, I mean before I met Lara ...

you walk down the street and no one was like, hey, you're from whatever. So it was like a nice kick in the ass to meet your daughter."

"It's too bad Lara's busy tonight," I said. I had been hoping that she would come with us to help ease along the conversation. I wasn't looking forward to spending an entire evening with Rowlf, even if it was for a good cause.

"She wants to stay home and hang out with her dad," Rowlf informed me.

Why did I felt uneasy?

"He won't hang out with anyone when he's writing," I said. "I hope she realizes that."

"Oh yeah, like, she ran it past him. Like, she said she wants to get to know him. Make up for lost time. He was, yeah, sure, maybe I do need a break."

Why did I feel even more uneasy?

Rowlf took my silence as encouragement for him to talk. "She really appreciates what you've done for her, gave her a wonderful childhood and all."

Wonderful childhood? When she fought like a caged cougar every step of the way?

"On that ranch. She liked it there, the horses, the dogs. And her stepfather. He was a real nice person, she says. I mean, he's still a nice person. He showed us a real good time, when we were down there. His wife is real nice, too. And Lara's brother. Good shit. We got along swell. Jeez, the way he can ride a horse and fork those bales of hay, it's really something. Like it struck me, he's a *useful* person. But getting back to her stepdad, he was very important to her during those childhood years, when she needed a father, like. But she *is* half Gully, genetically speaking, so she wants to explore that."

I was busy manoeuvring my vehicle through the sleet that slashed at the windshield. The wipers were having trouble removing it fast enough for me to see the road. Also, I was concerned about Lara. I hoped Gully would not be rude to her. He could be an insufferable prick, and especially when he was writing.

"Lara is so *family*," Rowlf was going on.

"Lara?" My voice cracked with incredulity.

"That's why she wanted to come home, to be part of her family. You must've raised her to value family. You should have seen her at that church camp. She was everybody's little mother. They all would go to her with their troubles. She really listens. Have you noticed how few people really listen?"

"I suppose…"

"You must be a wonderful person to have produced a daughter like Lara."

"No," I said, easing my foot carefully onto the brake pedal, slowing down to look for a parking spot. "No, I'm not a wonderful person."

The gallery was a full house, about twenty people sitting around uncomfortably on folding chairs. That was a good number for a literary reading. I could recall times when the audience numbered half a dozen and, once, when, apart from the reader, the host of the venue, and me as organizer, it consisted of the hovering shadow of a janitor who had to work the evening shift so someone would be there to lock up.

I had to admit to a bit of nostalgia – the musty building, the room with its podium and jug of water and assortment of poets, bards, and storytellers, the writers who passed through my life. The days of my youth were vividly returned to my senses, the thrill of those evenings when the literary world was new for me, the thrill of being near Harry. Harry attended all the readings, those of his students and his friends as well as his own. It was the best of times, although we didn't know it then. We were all struggling to be heard, to have an audience, to get a book published. We wished so ardently for the future and success. We had not yet learned that the best is when the promise is ahead, that reality can never live up to the dream.

The first reader of the evening was a young woman who read

a story about the sad experiences of a relationship. There was a poem about music deranged by longing. Somebody had a story about a kitten named Feathers and somebody else had a poem about wresting your freedom from those who won't let you have it. There was a poem about riding cold waves and sinking in the trough of the wind where memory and desire mix. I looked sideways towards Rowlf. He was listening intently, it appeared, concentrating on every word.

A very pretty seemingly modest young woman started to read a short story detailing her sexual experience with an older man, how he was old and gross and she was young and beautiful and how he replenished himself with her sweet plump flesh. The piece included much graphic material that she generously divulged without the slightest hint of embarrassment. I shrunk in my seat, but it didn't seem to bother anyone else.

The story was also excruciatingly slow moving. I decided that my time could be used more efficiently if I worked on my novel. In the week since I'd been wrapping myself around Harry and whispering in his ear, he had ... well, maybe blossomed is a little strong. But he no longer looked and felt like a corpse. He had traded the grey pallor for a kind of baby pinkness. He ate his soup like a good little boy without losing it all in the folds of his nightshirt. He still hadn't opened his eyes, but he was responding to my whispers with his own interspersed sighs. I fully expected that he would start to speak any day. The visiting nurse was pleased with the patient's progress. We made a ceremony of removing the IV. The Missing Persons Police were happy that soon they would be able to question him.

My novel, however, was basically the same one that Aunt Olive had trashed. Listening to that unabashed young woman on the podium, the thought came to me that maybe I *should* shake it up a bit. I could have the farm family break up and leave the farm. That might be the basis for a little more action. I could mine my own experiences on the ranch, experiences

Rowlf had brought back to my mind. Of course I would turn it into fiction. And I'd have to decide how far I wanted to go with the tall, dark, one-armed ranch hand who rode into the yard that hot summer day. For no one knew about him, no one, not even Aunt Olive, not my ex-husband, and especially not my youngest son.

I surfaced to find that the earnest young lady was still at it. I dived back under. I thought about Rowlf's remarks to me on the way to the gallery, how mistaken they were. If I was a wonderful person, I would have been there for people. I would not have allowed such distance to grow between Lara and me. Only the rattlesnake walks away from its young, as my mother, God rest her soul, used to say. But I did not walk away from Lara, I defended myself to myself. She chose a program offered at York. Maybe I was a bit too enthusiastic in my encouraging of her plan but I *had* to toss her out into the world, for her own good. But maybe I went overboard in my zeal to have her become an independent, functional individual. At the time, I had reasoned that I was responsible for that person being in the world, responsible for forcing her to grow up and take care of herself. But maybe it wasn't necessary to be so tough about it. Perhaps I had failed to recognize her emotional needs.

The reading showed no sign of ending or even slowing down. When I glanced around I discovered that what I had at first taken to be a large audience was, in fact, a large group of readers with a friend or lover in tow. As the evening droned on, nearly every one of those twenty people got up in turn and entertained us. But was not that exactly what I desired? The cure for Rowlf's writing bug – soul-destroying boredom.

On the drive home, Rowlf fairly bubbled over with enthusiasm. His comments included phrases about a social mosaic which becomes a literary mosaic, or was it vice versa, documentation of voices of the people, courage of individuals to reveal, root literature being like root music, such comments liberally spiked with "like," "y'know," "man," "rush," and such.

When we arrived back at the apartment, I was surprised to find that it was only nine-thirty. The quiet struck me. On the kitchen table was a note held down by a salt shaker informing Rowlf that Lara and her dad had gone out and would not be late. Rowlf immediately went to his room, without even stopping at the fridge. He said he wanted to get at it while the mood was with him. Or did he say muse? I too retired. I knew that due to the disturbing thoughts that had come to me at the reading, I wouldn't be able to sleep, but I also knew that the only solution was to deflect those thoughts from reality to fiction, or try. I sat down at my word processor and pressed the switch. I opened the file tentatively titled, *Sodbusters*, and read what I had written earlier that day.

'Under the bleak blustery August sky, the women were digging potatoes. Mavis and her children had come from the neighbouring homestead to help. Jenny, bent over her fork, glanced toward her friend. Mavis was wearing a baggy sweater and a floppy man's hat. She was on her knees, digging her rough hands into the black earth to make sure the children had not overlooked even one potato. Jenny recalled how, when she had first met Mavis, she had thought the other woman coarse and common, how she had compared the way Mavis set her table in such a haphazard manner on the bare wood with her own careful setting of cloth and cutlery. Now she felt remorse for her unkind thoughts and was filled with a sudden burst of love for her friend.

'Jenny set her face to her task. Laboriously, she put one foot up on the fork and pushed the tines into the dark moist soil. Suddenly, with the downward thrust of the muscles of her leg, a pain shot through her belly. She gasped and hung onto the shovel handle, waiting for the pain to subside. But then more pains followed, became rhythmic, wave upon wave of them, with no let up between. She could not stand. She collapsed to the ground. Mavis looked up from where she was, two rows over. Quickly, she got to her feet and moved toward Jenny.

"Let's get you into the house," she said.

"'No,' ground out Jenny. "I can't, can't stand. It's coming.""

"'Hey, you, Annie, you run to the house, quick now, and bring back some hot water from the reservoir, some clean cloths if you can find them, some scissors. Got that? Water, rags, scissors. And a sheet or blanket, too. Hurry it up girl. Don't dawdle, get a move on.""

'Jenny groaned as Mavis removed her sweater and placed it on the ground beneath her'."

Three pains in one paragraph ... what was another word for pain? And the last paragraph ... two hers, each referring to a different person, was confusing.

I felt thoroughly depressed, not because of the grammar and vocabulary, that could be easily fixed, but for the thing itself. Aunt Olive was right. Who wanted to read this stuff anymore? Books, movies, were full of car chases, serial killers, psychos, mashed metal, people sniffing cocaine, and especially weirdo sex. Nobody wanted to read page after page of descriptions of snowstorms, drought, getting hailed out, building log cabins, birthing babies in fields, strong friendships built out of hardships, the desperate life of the pioneer, even if you got into motives like what drove them to do it, even if you got into love stories. No one wanted to read about a time when there were no car chases because there were no cars, a time when the good guys outnumbered the bad guys.

Aunt Olive was right. I had to get myself out of that homesteader's shack.

Write about what you know – I was caught in my own words, words I had intoned year after year into the ears of students. I knew nothing, nothing exciting or important, anyway. My life had been that of a typical writer, dull, uneventful, mostly spent in front of a typewriter or computer in a room that was like a prison cell. Well, I said to myself, how about Papillon, or Jean Genet? Still, they had something to write about, Genet, his love story, shocking at the time, Papillon – solitary confinement,

Devil's Island, his ceaseless attempts to escape. A man who had spent most of his life in solitary confinement had more of a story to tell than I did. I groaned out loud.

Even if I traded in the homesteader's shack for the ranch, it wouldn't change much but the setting. I needed to bring the whole mess up to date. I needed new grist. Was it too late to have interesting experiences? Was it too late to get contemporary grist, sexual grist, for my mill? I thought about the pretty young woman at the reading. If she had the nerve to describe her sexual experiences, and with bad writing, then surely I could describe mine. But I hadn't had any lately, and my past experiences had not been all that exciting or kinky. Well, maybe a few, but they'd been so long ago, I couldn't remember. I needed new material. But where to get it? I didn't have that kind of male friend and my former husbands were out of the question since one was dead and one was happily remarried. Gully, I didn't even seriously consider. I might pick up someone if I went to a dance at the Kerby Centre with Aunt Olive and Fred, but I needed immediate inspiration.

I looked toward the stiff with whom I shared my bed. No, I shook my head. I would be crossing a forbidden boundary. Ours had never been nor was it meant to be a physical relationship. Such an act would disrupt the universe. Whispering in his ear had been hard enough. How could I possibly take it a step further?

I talked sternly to myself. You have to do it. Your novel is at stake. I walked to my side of the bed and sat myself down on top of the covers.

I realized almost immediately that this was going to be a real challenge, not only because one of the principals was comatose but because the other had serious mental and emotional restrictions concerning what was about to take place. In my day, and what I remembered about relationships, there was an unspoken expectation that a man should please a woman. It was up to him to make her moan. The reason for this, as I understood it, was that men are so easily pleased, the woman doesn't even have to try. In fact, if she tries too hard it can be bad news. If I remembered correctly, it was like playing with a firecracker. You had to treat it with kid gloves or it would explode. Obviously, I had quite a different problem on, or shall I say 'in', my hands. If I was going to bring this head to life, I was going to have to pleasure it with a vengeance. I, who had always been a shy woman, was going to have to be bold. My novel demanded it.

Another realization was that before anything of a seductive nature could happen, I would have to get naked. It didn't help that Harry was comatose. I had too many memories of his eyes traveling up and down a woman's frame, any woman's frame. The fact was, I would be a sixty-year-old woman stripping before a man for the first time in ... I thought ... seven years. No, I yelled to myself. I tried to blank out my brain – things drooping and sagging, bulging where they shouldn't and not bulging where they should. It was just too awful. I remembered an article I read once about how you shouldn't care if certain parts of your body are jiggling, as long as you're having a good time. Shake what your mamma gave you, I believe was the mantra. But that wasn't my nature. At my first sexual encounter, my first marriage, my first wedding night, I'd taken off my clothes in the closet. Gully had later used the episode, adjusted only slightly, in one of his hilarious novels. As for my other marriages, I had always let the current husband take the initiative, which is what we did in my day, unbelievable as that may seem today.

This called for a good stiff drink. I looked toward the bureau. There sat my hot toddy bottle of brandy. 'Come', 'come', it seemed to beckon. I went into the bathroom and returned with my toothbrush glass. I poured a good measure of the brandy into the glass and, sitting prim and straight on the edge of the bed, drank it down in one fell swoop. When my head and my thoughts stopped whirling, I was sans sweater and bra.

I slipped down my slacks and scurried under the covers. A moment later, my panties appeared in a tossed arc landing in a sad little heap on the carpet.

I lay stiff and still on my side of the bed and waited for him to do something. Then I remembered – the article said that it was no fun for a man if the woman hides under the covers and is uncomfortable with their visually exploring each other's bodies. I reached one arm down to where I had deposited the brandy bottle on the floor. This time I drank straight from the flask. It seemed more efficient. Besides, I couldn't remember where I had set down the glass.

Thus fortified, like a good little soldier, I threw aside the blanket, the sheet, and, without meaning to, the pile of useless printout that had collected on Harry's side of the bed, the files and stacks of papers that had become scenes and chapters of failed manuscript, the pages I had expected him to infuse with inspiration. I looked at the confused mess on the floor. In the immortal words of Scarlett O'Hara, I'd think about it tomorrow. Now I had work to do.

I unbuttoned Harry's pyjama top, pulled one end of the neat bow tied around his waist, pulled his pyjama bottoms down, not easy, since, in spite of his loss of weight, Harry was still a large man, large bones, large frame. I slipped my hand down between his thighs. There I found winter reincarnated. I fiddled around a bit, using both the massaging motion and the trickling fingers motion, both of which I had read about in that article. Nothing. I wondered about a heating blanket, a hot water bottle. I looked up and around in despair. I turned back and looked down. I had never seen such a pitiful shrivelled small white curled up cock in my entire life. I bent over it. I put my hot brandy-flavoured tongue on its tip. Nothing. I licked my tongue along it length. Nothing. I must be doing something wrong, I surmised. According to the articles, that was supposed to work. Again, I was a totally inadequate failure. Was there nothing I could do right?

I became angry. What in hell did Harry think he was doing, lying there day in and day out, expecting everything to be done for him, doing nothing to earn his keep? Why was I the one who had to tell him the story? He should be telling me the story. Why was I trying so hard to please him when he wasn't trying to please me? Why was I thinking that I was not an object of pleasure? Why was I trying so hard to give him pleasure? What about my pleasure? He was the man, he was supposed to make me feel good.

With that thought firmly in mind, I straddled his body with my thighs. I stuffed that soft flabby appendage into me, holding it tight where it would do the most good. Thus mounted, I slowly rode the beast to my ultimate pleasure.

10.

―――❈―――

TODAY WILL BE YOUR CRAZIEST WORKDAY in a long time. The tides are turning, and it's better to turn with them than to stand with your hand outstretched trying to stop progress. I was reading my horoscope and working up a sweat on the treadmill. Skinny arms pumping, I was wearing myself out and getting nowhere. "Like life itself." I spoke it aloud. The person on the neighbouring treadmill turned her head sharply toward me and just about fell off. You have to look straight ahead when you're on those machines. That, too, was like life. Maybe I would use that in my novel, the metaphor about the treadmill. I marvelled at the way metaphors, ideas, scenes had been jumping into my pocket the last couple of days since my showdown with Harry. Finally, finally, the writing was going well. Finally, I knew how to write my book. Finally, I was in control. I had made some major decisions – it would be two hundred and fifty pages, no more, no less. Oh, I had a long and winding road ahead of me. That goes without saying. A novel is a lengthy process.

I felt a little bad about abandoning Jenny. Maybe I'll go back to her someday, I told myself to assuage my guilt. But now, *now*, I had other fish to fry. The big picture had been revealed to me while I straddled the loins of Harry. I would write my autobiography. The rule for storytelling was that the main character has to have a problem. Fine and dandy – got lots of those. My only conundrum was which one to choose.

My first marriage happened so long ago, I no longer viewed it as a problem, at least an emotional one. The anger I still felt toward Gully had to do with his theft of my work. The other stuff – the pain of loss and abandonment, the sadness caused by his betrayal – seemed to have happened to someone in a film I had seen a long time ago of which I could not remember the details. Okay, what about my last marriage? Not much there. Not enough angst. Parties, hobnobbing with the ski crowd. It was a hilarious ride the short while it lasted. Then there was the good man in the Foothills. Thinking of him brought me to the one-armed bandit. Yes, I would write about him. Finally, that story would be told. The mysterious stranger who had been riding the rodeo circuit with his one good arm, who needed work for the winter, who by happenstance had been drinking in the same bar as Harry one golden September afternoon. I would write the love story I found in his empty sleeve.

I gave a great deal of consideration to starting at the beginning and working toward the end, thus incorporating my complete history, but the thought of plodding through the details of all those years defeated me before I even got started. I decided, instead, to start at the end. My main character was going to commit suicide because she has recently turned sixty, is faced with her mortality, and feels that her life has been a total failure. Then her plan is foiled because she stumbles upon a man's head sticking up out of the snow and this helicopter is looking for him and finds her also. That would lead into the next scene, which naturally, would be in a hospital. Then she takes the head home and tries to nurse it back to life. Meanwhile, her former husband shows up, as well as her daughter. I didn't know what was going to happen next but felt confident that things would fall into place. Nor did I yet know the ending; it was much too soon for that. However, I did know some rules for the ending. Years ago, I attended a writing lecture in our city given by a famous novelist – have a smash-up ending, he said. Also, the ending has to come out of the characters and not be superimposed as a *deus ex machina*. It must be plausible but not predictable. The main character has to change and grow. Hallelujah! I had already done that by getting on top of Harry, by tossing aside my modesty along with my panties. The coward had performed an act of bravery, the prude at heart had come out of the closet.

All these great ideas were pumping to my brain along with a rush of oxygen. As soon as I got back to my apartment, I would go to my room and get them all down. Thank you Aunt Olive for introducing me to the fitness centre. Physical fitness was a wonderful thing.

It was then I spotted Ms. Pogo Stick and Fred.

The exercise machines were in front of a large window wall that looked down into the street, providing a diversion to keep exercisers from expiring from boredom while they were going nowhere. It was like watching television, only you had to make up your own script. On the sidewalk, bundles of clothes that I could only assume were human beings, were scurrying along – we were in the throes of yet another cold snap. Across the street, in front of the Higher Ground coffee shop, an old man was stomping his feet in an arthritic manner. I realized with a bit of a start that it was Fred, although there was no reason why it should not be Fred, given that he lived in the neighbourhood. But, then, who should come along but Ms. Pogo Stick, wearing a mini skirt, short jacket and leggings up to here, flaunting her body in the face of the elements. She slid to a stop in front of Fred, real close, and that's when I noticed her shoes – red with high thin heels and ankle strap. I gasped. She'd been tracking Fred right into the bowels of our building! She must have got the wrong floor! My floor!

For a few moments, the couple engaged in what appeared to be lively hilarious conversation. I could feel her physical intensity across space and through the window. My heart sank. What chance did my dear sweet old Aunt Olive have in the face of that vibrant youth? They disappeared into the coffee shop.

What to do? It wasn't a question. I didn't even try to resist. I stopped the treadmill, jumped off, grabbed my horoscope and my hooded warm-up jacket from off the floor, pulling the jacket over my head and stuffing my arms into the sleeves as I ran down the stairs and out the door. I hurried across the street, then slowed as I sidled into Higher Ground, holding my hood close to my face. But I didn't have to worry. Fred and Legs, so renamed in my brain, were in a huddle in a back corner near the fireplace, foreheads nearly touching across a small table, so totally engrossed in each other, I was able to order my coffee and carry it to a nearby table without being spotted. Positioning myself behind Fred, I kept my head down and my ears open.

It was no use. The din in the place scarcely allowed table mates to hear each other, let alone eavesdroppers. Only a scattered *and* or *but* came through. But if appearances meant anything, the conversation was hot and heavy. Hands clasped, attention riveted, it was obvious – those two were engaged in love talk.

I couldn't drink my coffee. My stomach was a raw wound. Poor Aunt Olive. After a lifetime of drudgery and hardship on the farm, after the death of Uncle Owen to whom she had been devoted, after the heartbreak of raising six children, one of whom had drowned in the slough at age ten, she had found new happiness with Fred. And now, this.

It was then I spotted, on the other side of their table, the square firm countenance of Rock hiding behind a newspaper. I hadn't been imagining it then! In spite of him telling me that the case was closed, he seemed to be still around – in the stairwells, in the shadows outside my door, I felt his presence in the empty spaces. When I was going through the apple bin at the neighbourhood market, when I was waiting for the walk light to turn green, when I was entering my building, I felt the force of his eyes watching me from the shrubbery of his brows. I had decided that these weird feelings were originating in my mind and were in no real way connected to him. I told myself that he was coincidentally at Higher Ground for a morning coffee like everyone else, but I didn't believe myself. There was something so cloak and daggerish in the way he held that paper up, the way he glanced around it from time to time, toward Legs and Fred. But why would he be shadowing them? Had the case been reopened? Even if it had, what did Fred and Legs have to do with it?

I took the long way out of the cafe so that I could walk past him. Deliberately, I jostled his newspaper. I wanted him to know that he wasn't fooling me. I was on to his game, whatever it was.

Distracted and worried about Aunt Olive, I returned to my apartment and was reaching into the fridge for a juice to refuel my depleted fluids when I felt the presence of Lara like a cold wind at my back. She had been doing that for the past week, ambushing me, maybe because Rowlf wasn't around much. Was something wrong in the relationship? Dare I hope? But, truth to tell, I was becoming fond of the little guy. He had such a damned cute quirky smile.

When I had asked her about Rowlf, all she had said was "he's out," which had inspired me to ask the further question, "What happened to his plan of concocting the evening meal?"

"If that's the way you feel, I'll do it," she had snapped.

"You will not," I had stated. "It's my kitchen."

The result of Rowlf's absence was that Lara had more hassle time on her hands. She would waylay me in the dusky hallway, she would suddenly pop around the frame of the kitchen doorway, she would corner me in the bathroom when my mouth was full of foam and dental floss. "Let's talk," she'd say. What she really meant was, let's review your case, let's list the charges, let's see if you can get out of this one. I presumed sentencing would come later. If I tried to capitulate or agree with her, she wouldn't have it. She demanded that I defend myself, which acted as a reference grid upon which she could create ever escalating charges, building to a climax of condemnation. Under the guise of family issues, she replayed all the hurts, arrows, slings, every goddamned little detail that she could dredge up out of what I had always thought was a fairly normal childhood – "You smashed my Iron Maiden," "You made me wear new jeans to school." No good to explain that I had a horrendous migraine that day or that new jeans can't become old jeans until you wear them.

The whole business was exhausting. Why is it that when people want to talk it's always about unpleasant things. Lots of pleasant things happened in our lives too – watching a foal being born on a spring morning in a field of crocuses peeping through a light fall of snow. Lara and I held hands while my ranch hand with his one dexterous arm helped the mare. I could still feel her child's hand in mine, fear and wonder in the grip. But do people/children want to talk about things like that? The answer is a big fat NO.

But surprise, surprise. As I was fumbling in the fridge for the juice, I heard, "You look tired. How about if I make you a hot drink?" She slid closed the kitchen door, which should have alerted me, which did alert me, but I staunchly squared my shoulders. Why did I think it was my maternal duty to let myself be trashed by a child whose method of connecting with family was to get it out of her system and into mine? Why couldn't I be like a friend of mine who, when his children took him to task, told them to go out and see if they could get themselves adopted. Instead, I let Lara make me a cup of tea.

From my chair at the kitchen table, into which I had despondently sunk, I watched Lara's brisk movements as she turned to the stove. Since her return, the most remarkable change had come over her. The immaculately groomed attractive young woman with little makeup, a turtle neck sweater and slacks and jacket would not have been out of place in a corporate office. "Can I ask you something?" she said, filling the kettle.

I could feel the tension in the small bones in the back of my neck. I rolled my head on my shoulders. "Sure. What?"

"Well, I was just wondering. Why *did* you break up with Daddy?"

"Hmmm." I tried to think of a plausible answer. In memory, his infidelity seemed inconsequential.

"I mean, he seems like a nice guy."

Something held me back from revealing the story of the stolen manuscript. She was, after all, his child. She embodied his genes.

"Was it because of his affairs?"

"Affairs?"

"They weren't really affairs, you know. Little flirtations, one night stands. He couldn't help it, the way women chased him, very attractive, *young* women. He was only human. And he *was* an artist. He needed inspiration."

"I see."

"He truly cared for you. He told me." By now Lara was pouring boiling water over tea bags in a pot. "He admits he shouldn't have slept around but...," she hesitated, "you were cold."

God give me strength, I whispered to myself and thought the better part of valour would be to say nothing.

"You haven't answered my question," said Lara.

I looked up across the table. Her blue eyes were like the piercing light of a police interrogation room. I thought of Rock.

"He didn't see me," I said, knowing that what I was about to say was going to sound lame to someone who hadn't lived it. "He only saw me as an extension of himself."

"And *that* broke up your marriage?" She fairly shrieked.

"Shhh," I pointed a thumb in the general direction of Gully's corner in the other room. "You don't think it's important to be a person, an individual?"

"Of course it is. But Daddy would have worked it out with you ... if you'd told him how you felt. That's the sort of person he is."

I kept my mouth shut so I wouldn't screech obscenities.

"I just want to ask you one question." Lara brought the tea to the table.

"Yes."

"Was it fair of you to deprive me of my father just because of some silly petty problem on your part? Was your stubbornness and pride more important than my childhood?"

I looked into those incredibly steady, startling eyes. "I don't know," I answered. I was alarmed at my response. As much as a few weeks ago, I would have raged in denial, at least answered testily and smart-assedly. But now I thought about the question. I would have to think about it further.

For a few minutes, it seemed Lara felt that she had worked me over enough for one day. But there was more. "If only you hadn't shot Nelly," she said quietly, staring at the table.

"Nelly? She was run over by a truck!"

"And then you shot her."

"She was writhing in agony!"

"We could have taken her to a vet."

"The vet was at least an hour away. We couldn't even move her. The vet would have put her down."

"You don't know that."

"The whole of her hindquarters was broken."

"It wasn't so much that you did it, but that you *could* do it."

"Somebody had to do it. No one else was there."

"In that instant, you changed for me."

I thought a while. Was that when Lara had become an impossible adolescent?

"You made me run to the house and get the shotgun. You *involved* me."

She was right. "In the chaos of the moment, a person has to make a quick decision. Perhaps I thought it would be easier for you to get the gun while I stayed with Nelly. I don't know. I can't remember!" It was a cry in the dark.

"You were so tough. So heartless. It was scary. My mother was a monster."

"I wouldn't be here if I wasn't tough. When you were born, I was alone. I made a vow to myself that we'd survive." I stopped. Had I said too much? Would she think me a whining wimp? And maybe survival wasn't the most important thing. Maybe how you survived counted, too. The saying was, when the pillow is being pressed over your face, you don't stop to ask questions. But maybe you should. Maybe you should. "Tough people suffer too," I said.

Lara went back to her room where she was sorting the family trunk, much of which consisted of her maternal grandmother's notes and photos and scrapbooks. Lara had been especially close to my mother. After the divorce, we had lived with her. She had taken care of Lara while I got a degree in education, figuring that would give me a career upon which to raise a child and get my life more or less sorted out.

I was left to ponder. Perhaps my destiny was to not have a relationship with my children, or anybody else for that matter. Perhaps my fatal flaw was that even though I felt that I loved deeply, even though I thought my strong point was my ability to love, perhaps I could not show my love to those I loved most dearly. I thought of a recent exchange with Lara – "I loved you." "You never loved me." I thought of Lara's stepfather on the ranch who had accused me of being intelligent. Maybe it wasn't his fault that he didn't know about my love. Perhaps I was the only one who did know. Perhaps I had not revealed to Gully this ability.

Thirty years ago, I convinced myself that Gully would not want to know about Lara, that he would not be interested in the fact that he had a child in the world. I convinced myself that I was protecting her against being hurt. Now I wondered if I had wanted to punish him and that was my way of doing it. Perhaps it *was* a matter of pride. I didn't know. I never would know because the issues were buried too deeply in the past.

Sessions with Lara always wiped me out, a condition that is not conducive to the creative process. But I was determined to get to my writing – I had already wasted an hour spying on Fred and Legs and another one talking with Lara. I wanted to take advantage of the current inspirational wave I was riding.

If I had a close relationship with anyone on earth, it was with Harry, that is, when things were going good, as they were now. Perhaps the tragedy of my life was that over a span of so many years we had coincided so infrequently. Or perhaps the beauty of our relationship was the infrequency of it. At any rate, as winter bared its teeth for one last attack against the windowpanes, Harry and I were safe in our cozy haven of pleasure. He was my home place. When I lay beside him and put my arms around him, I was child again, with a child's sense of wonder and confidence of future. When I curled into the comfort of him and put my head into the curve of his sheltering shoulder, when I listened to his murmurings in my ear, I knew the mystery that resided in the deepest layer of life itself and the hope of glory days stretching interminably into the future. His variety never ceased to motivate me. Sometimes he would lie still and straight, breathing quietly. Sometimes, he would become excited, twitching and jumping as though he were being given electric shocks. Sometimes he would frown with concentration. Sometimes, something almost like a smile would appear on his face. Sometimes, his whole body would shake with some contained mirth, which, in turn, would cause me to laugh. Sometimes, he would droop with melancholy, causing me, also, a great sadness. Sometimes, I could feel tears scalding his eyelids and my own eyes would burn with anguish.

Thus, I dreamed his dreams of landscape and thus began again to know myself, a person I realized had become a stranger. Although he did not speak, he freed my voice to speak. Since I could hear his thoughts, I knew what he was saying and every word was amazing. I studied him with unwavering eyes, with insatiable curiosity. I was able to sense all of his moods. I listened to all he had to tell me. And sometimes I would feel that he was stroking my head as if I truly were a child and I would embrace him even more tightly and press myself even more lovingly against him. After a while, I would get up from where I was lying beside him and attach myself to my computer where the words flowed like liquid gold.

But that eventful morning, our communion was not meant to be. No sooner had Lara left me, an emotional wreck to contemplate my past mistakes, than Aunt Olive dropped in. Drat, thought I, when I opened the door and saw her standing in the hall. Fond as I was of Aunt Olive, I did not want to see her just then. She was certain to discern something in my manner of what I had witnessed at the coffee house. But I had to let her in. I could see right away that she was in trouble. She was still wearing her robe, which was half open, sash dangling in a loose knot somewhere around her thighs. A crumpled, stained nightgown could be seen in the opening. Her hair was a wild bird's nest and above her down-at-the-heel slippers, her blotchy varicose-veined legs were evident. I could smell whisky. I reached out an arm and drew her quickly into the apartment before Schmidt or anyone else could see her.

While I was brewing up a pot of coffee, Aunt Olive said to my back, "What's up?"

"I was going to ask you the same thing," I countered.

"No, I mean what's up?" Her voice was not slurred. I guessed most of the whisky had been soaked up by her nightgown.

"What do you mean?" I returned.

"You look different."

"How?"

"Don't go all coy on me. I can tell when a woman's getting some."

"Some?" I turned a quizzical face.

"Okay, if that's the way you want to play it. I only hope it isn't that guy behind the curtain. I'd be real disappointed if you went back to him. He never was worth it, never will be."

"Why don't you like Gully?" I put in quickly, clutching at the turn in the conversation. "You never liked him."

"Tricky dicky," she said. "Too clever by far."

"He seems to have turned over a new leaf. He's been working like crazy for the last two months."

"I thought you gave him six weeks."

"He asked for an extension. He said he wanted to see how things turn out."

"What things."

"In his novel. He wants to see how it ends."

"I'd be careful if I were you. I wouldn't trust that guy any further than I can throw him. Anyway," she said, lighting up the first of what I knew would be half a dozen cigarettes, "glad somebody is."

"What?" Somehow, I had missed a page.

"Glad your love life is tickety boo. Mine is the shits."

Oh, oh, I thought. Here it comes.

"That egotistical maniac. That swelled headed excuse for a man."

"Fred?"

"He makes me sick. Some floozy makes eyes at him and he thinks she means it. Christ, the ego of some men."

"It doesn't mean anything," I said. "He's just having a bit of fun. Flirting makes him feel young again."

The coffee was finished dripping. I got two cups out of the cupboard.

"He'd drop his pants for anything that comes along."

A thin, wavering quality in Aunt Olive's voice caused me to look her way. She was blinking her eyes quickly. I was shocked. I had never seen Aunt Olive like that before in my entire life. She must have sensed my scrutiny. She pulled herself together.

"It's the boobs," she said, her voice taking on an edge. "Fred's a boobs man. Mine sag."

I directed my gaze to her boobs. I wanted to say, they look great, but truth to tell, they did appear to be rather low. "Everybody's does," I said instead. "That's what boobs do, they hang. Don't let anybody tell you any different."

"Her's don't."

"They will. Time's on your side. Anyway, maybe they do. We haven't seen her without her sports bra."

"No matter how you look at it, hers don't sag as much as mine."

"Of course they don't. Yours have had fifty years of living more than hers. You've birthed and nurtured six kids. Be proud of what your boobs have done in this life. Here, drink this, you'll feel better." I set a cup of coffee on the table before her. She drank like a horse at the trough after a tough day in the field. When she spoke again, it was in the feisty voice I recognized. "At least my boobs are all mine. Hah! That hair piece masquerading as Lothario."

"Hair piece?"

"I've never told even you, because I knew it was a matter of pride with him, but underneath all that hair he's bald as a billiard ball."

"Really?" I tried to imagine Fred without hair.

"The measure of the man, vain as a peacock. Shallow as all get out."

"You know how men are. Like dogs who chase a fire engine but wouldn't know what to do if they caught one."

"It isn't as though I haven't tried. Christ, the things I've done for that man."

"It will all sort itself out." Clichés, I thought. Have I nothing better to offer than clichés? At my age and a writer?

"I paid a fortune for black lacy underwear that scratched like hell … the lace. I surprised him by wearing a trench coat with nothing on underneath."

"What?"

"For a romantic evening. I met him at the door. I had a bottle of champagne."

A response escaped me, although niggling at the back of my mind, was the question of whether that might be where I had gone wrong in my love life.

"I've made up my mind. I'm gonna write her a letter. There's a few things she should know. Like, how long it takes him to get it up. Like, you have to move fast before it disappears."

"I'll get you another cup of coffee."

By the time Aunt Olive left, she seemed to be feeling slightly better.

"Promise me you'll take a shower and put your face on," I said at the door.

"What does it matter? There's no one to see me."

"I'm going to see you. I'm coming over later and...," for a despairing moment I thought about Harry, "we're going shopping." I hated shopping.

As I closed the door, I couldn't help but wonder about Legs. What was her motive in pursuing Fred? His money? Lots of old guys had more money than Fred. His body? I couldn't believe that, especially since viewing those beautiful young hunks in the weight room. To be sure, it was puzzling.

11.

⸺✸⸺

LARA WAS KNEELING ON THE FLOOR before my mother's trunk, her torso bending and rising as in a prayer ritual. Her long hair in its restored state turned out to be a lovely delicate blonde, a luminescent veil hiding her profile. The trunk gaped open like a desecrated body, all its intimate contents stacked in neat little piles on the carpet or in the lid. Like a magician, Lara reached in a graceful arm and pulled out a shoebox. In that shoe box would be photographs, all I had kept of my share of the thousands my mother had taken during her life, beginning with a box camera in the early days, ending in her last years with some super model complete with gadgets. I thought of how she had loved to have slide shows after Sunday dinner and how we would gather in the living room for that purpose and how impatient I had often felt at those times. She had neatly catalogued her slides and photos and filed them in metal cases and albums. After her death, they were sorted and distributed to appropriate family members. Where were all those slides and photos now? Had the others even kept them? Did anyone ever look at them? Or were they hidden away in the back of a cupboard, or in a trunk in a spare room?

I was leaning on a doorframe, defending myself as usual. "Other mothers were back in the work force before their kids were in kindergarten. How was going back to school any different?"

Which was in response to: "You always put him first. You were always running off to lectures, every time he was in town." Of course, she meant Harry. What would she say, do, if she knew that, as she spoke those words, he was in the apartment, in my bed, separated from her room, the spare bedroom, by only a bathroom and short hallway?

"You were always locked in your room writing a paper or a poem for his class," she responded to my question.

Which evoked my: "That's not true. I always came out to get a good dinner on the table. I always put you and your brothers first."

"Yeah, put us in ballet class or crafts or soccer. So we were out of the way while you went about your gadding."

"Gadding! That's what you call working my ass off. You write a dissertation, see how easy it is. You sell your soul to the teaching life. See how it bleeds you dry."

"Just so you could be near him... "

Every minute I was chasing Harry I felt that I was betraying life. Every minute I was living I felt that I was betraying Harry. See how easy that is, I wanted to scream. To live the schizophrenic life. But I kept quiet, because she would say, why didn't you tell Harry to go to hell. And I would have to say, "I couldn't."

In spite of this serve/return exchange, things were looking up between Lara and me. The last few discussions between us were different, not so much in content as in voice. Lara's new voice was quiet, her tone thoughtful, even reflective. Maybe she was wearing down. Maybe her interest was redirected toward plans for her wedding in the spring. The wedding seemed to be still on, in spite of the fact that Rowlf was living a double life. He'd come home in the early morning, crash, then leave again in the afternoon. Sometimes, he didn't come home at all. I wondered if he was working a night shift. "You might call it that," Lara said when questioned, but she didn't provide me with details.

The thought occurred to me that spending hours every day going through my mother's trunk had a calming effect on my daughter. Maybe that was what had caused her to want a church wedding. Or had her decision to have a traditional wedding motivated her to sort through the trunk? All I knew was that a new Lara was evolving.

"Anyway, we're not talking about other mothers," said Lara with her new voice. "We're talking about you."

We certainly were. And it was my fault. When making my way down the hall to the linen closet, I had noticed Lara's open door. I had leaned against the frame and whispered, "what're you doing?"– a phrase it took me only minutes to regret.

Although it had started innocently enough. "Those diaries of grandmother's." Lara looked toward one of the piles on the carpet. "They're incredible."

My eyes followed the direction of her gaze. At the time of my mother's death, I had skimmed through them and, quite frankly, found them boring, page after page after page of doing laundry, having a migraine, attending a church meeting.

"The contents, a woman's life, the sheer volume of detail." Lara looked up at me with those shooting star eyes. "An invisible woman desperate to be visible. Grandmother felt compelled to document a non-life to give herself a life. So she'd know she existed in this world. Like those prairie women who staked a shirt on a post to see the wind, so they'd know it was real and not in their heads."

"You know that?"

"My major *was* Canadian literature." She looked at me curiously. "I suppose you don't know that."

I was sure I had known it at one time. The fact that I'd forgotten may sound like careless parenting but she had changed her major several times.

"Yes, I do."

"No, you don't."

"It just slipped my mind. That was several years ago."

That was when the conversation deteriorated to my parenting rating, which Lara considered off the bottom of the chart.

"Oh, I don't care for myself any more." Lara paused. "I feel sorry for the boys."

"You don't know what you're talking about. You haven't been here. Richard loves the ranch. He plans to take it over eventually. Normally, he comes into town on a week-end or I go there. This has been such a strange winter, and then all this snow. But Alice and I get along splendidly. I'm happy for Dad, that he found someone who suits him. Your other two brothers are doing what they want to do. Why would I hold them back?"

"They had to get their own lunch."

"What?"

Up until then, we had been speaking quietly because of Gully. "Shhh," said Lara. "When you went back to university."

I closed the door. "They didn't come home for lunch! You all took the school bus to town."

"They had to come home after school to an empty house."

"I was there most of the time. I arranged my classes so I would be. Besides, you were there. You were fifteen. Their father was there."

"He was out in the barn."

"It was within shouting distance of the house!"

"In spring he was busy with the branding." Before I could respond to that missile, she continued. "Whenever he came along, wandering in out of the cold from some misadventure with some woman, you gave him the best bed in the spare room."

"There was only one bed in the spare room. We were friends."

"Umm, hmmm."

"We talked. That's what we did together. Talk. We had something to say to each other. That's rare, you know, two people who have something to say to each other." I took a deep breath. "I never slept with him."

"What's sex compared to slavish devotion?"

"Dad knew we were friends. He didn't mind."

"He did mind. You just never cared whether or not he minded. And how about that cowboy with one arm?"

The switch in topic caught me off guard. "What cowboy?"

"You know perfectly well 'what cowboy.' How many cowboys have one arm? Do you think I was stupid? Do you think kids don't notice?"

"Whatever you noticed, your imagination was working overtime."

"I noticed because I was in love with him, too. The way little girls are. He was such a romantic figure. A rodeo champion and all."

I thought fast. "You projected your feelings onto me."

"I blamed you for him leaving."

"You blamed me for everything."

"Dad. You made him leave, too."

"He didn't leave. I did. Anyway, you were away at school by then. How do you know what happened?"

"I just know. I know you and I know Dad. Dad's a team player. You aren't."

How could I tell her that we simply outgrew each other? She would think that equally feeble as my excuse for breaking up with Gully.

"He's happier with Alice," I said. "They have a lot in common. He wasn't happy with me." No one is, I thought.

"You were my life," I said. "You and your brothers. I didn't resent that life. I was not one of those career mothers who resent their children. I accepted that, until you were older, I was doomed to frustration. In the meantime, I tried to keep everybody happy. Obviously I kept no one happy. That is the tragedy of my life."

"Oh, stop being melodramatic."

"I just don't see why we have to keep rehashing all this stuff. We can't bring back the past. It's over and done with."

"You may be done with the past," murmured Lara, "but maybe the past isn't done with you."

I sighed. "Why do you want to quarrel with me?"

"I'm not quarrelling. I just want to sort out what happened. I want to be unconfused."

We were silent. I was thinking. Perhaps I *should* tell her more of the story.

"I discovered your father…," I started, then realized that, although muffled and distant, I could hear the rhythmic tapping of Gully's keyboard, like morse code from a war zone. It struck me. If we could hear him typing, he could hear us talking. I looked at the door. It had slipped its latch and was open a few inches. Panic rose up in my chest. What had we been talking about? Quickly, I closed the door, firmly this time, although he knew the story I was about to tell since he had been there.

I turned back to Lara. The way she was kneeling in jeans and shirt, she could have been fifteen again. I so wished she were, wished that we could start over and try to do better, try not to make the same mistakes. But she was a thirty-year-old woman. She had a right to know the story.

"I discovered Gully … your father," I started again, "when I was teaching creative writing at Mount Royal College. I had already published two small collections and he was running a submarine outlet. I used to drop in to his place for a bite to eat before going to teach my evening class. We got to talking. I told her about my class, about writing. Hey, he said, that sounds interesting. Maybe I should give it a try. A few weeks later, he coyly confessed a partial first draft of a novel. I politely expressed interest. He wondered if I would look at it. I did and performed the necessary grunts of approval." I paused, trying to remember what came next. Why, in fact, had we got married? Likely, I had not loved him. No doubt I had been in love with him. When I forced my mind to it, I recalled a lot of twirly lights and razzle dazzle. I have to say, I couldn't really recall the sex, but my overall impression was that it was okay.

"I introduced him to Harry," I said. "They became great friends. That's when his writing took off."

Lara was sitting back on her heels, obliquely studying my face, watching my mouth, absorbing each word that came out of it. Her face contained a mixture of wariness and hope. She wanted a love story. She wanted to believe that her parents had loved each other and that out of that great love she had been born.

It was quiet in the room. The silence was waiting for me to break it.

"You were the most important thing in my life."

"You never told me."

"You should have known without being told."

"Nobody knows without being told, that's what words are for."

Fortunately, I didn't have to make up a version of the love story of Lara's parents because at that moment the phone rang, muffled and distant. I could have let it ring, but I was thankful for the interruption. I flung open the door and hurried down the hall to where my own disembodied voice was coming from the cushions of the living room sofa. "I'll get back to you as soon as possible," it said. But the person at the other end didn't leave a message. Instead, the phone, now in my hand, rang again.

I pressed the talk button. Before I had a chance to say hello, my ear was bombarded with chaos. A male voice was yelling, "stop, don't do that! Stop!" There was a crash, a cry of pain, a voice saying "no, no," then wailing in the background. I threw the phone back into the sofa cushions and made a dash for the doorway. Not stopping to wait for the elevator, I lunged down the stairwell and burst into Aunt Olive's apartment just as she was about to pull the trigger.

I slid to a stop and made my voice low and quiet. "Aunt Olive, it's okay, it's going to be all right. Just take it easy." Thus murmuring, I inched closer to the crouched figure standing solid, tensed and ready for action. The gun was pointed straight at Fred's balls. At least, I assumed it was Fred. I didn't recognize the bald dome.

"She yanked off my hair piece," Fred said. "And then she had this gun. Jesus, I didn't even know she owned a gun."

"Aunt Olive… " I reached out my arm

"Get out of the way." Her voice was tough as cowhide. "I don't want you to get hurt."

"Come on, Aunt Olive, this isn't the way to resolve problems."

"I'm gonna plug the sunovabitch full of holes and then I'm gonna wipe the floor with him."

I suddenly realized that no one was going to take that gun away from Aunt Olive. It would have to be her idea to give it up.

"But then you're going to go to jail," I reasoned. "Is he worth it?"

For a moment, we were all exceptionally still. Then Aunt Olive slid her eyes in my direction. "You're right," she said. "No goddamn man is worth it." She handed me the gun. "Here, take it so I'm not tempted again." With that she collapsed on the couch and began to sob. I stood over her, totally astounded at the change from pistol-packing momma to soft quivering femininity.

Fred gently pushed me out of the way and crouched before her. "Come on now sweetie, you know it's you I love. There, there, cuddle bun. She's not near as pretty as you. Nobody's as pretty as you."

From the doorway I looked back at the two of them, Fred cradling her in his arms, she looking over his shoulder giving me the wink.

Life was truly an amazing thing.

In the doorway I bumped into Lara. She must have followed me and witnessed the scene. I widened my eyes and lifted my eyebrows and indicated that we should leave. I closed the door softly behind us.

"Wow," said Lara.

"Yeah."

"Doesn't it ever get any better? Don't people ever get their problems worked out?"

Lara saved me from having to answer by following her question with a statement. "It's so sad, what happens to people. Aunt Olive was so beautiful when she was young. There's pictures in Granny's shoe box."

"Beauty is no insurance against what might happen to you in this life." Thinking I should be safe with that piece of blatant banality, I went on. "Besides, she's still beautiful. Fred thinks she's beautiful."

"Does he? Or was he just trying to make her feel better?"

"He thinks so."

"I wonder if she has diaries and scrapbooks."

"Not everyone keeps a diary. Or scrapbooks."

"Not everyone is like Granny. I remember how we used to make scrapbooks together. I remember sitting at her kitchen table and cutting out pictures with those little blunt-edged scissors. She always had a stack of old magazines and we'd cut out pictures of tulips and daffodils and Campbell's soup and I remember a huge butterfly and there were always lots of pictures of mothers and daughters and I used to cut those out and pretend the little girls were me and the mothers were you. And I remember Sunday School papers and the pictures of Jesus with his lambs and we'd glue those into the scrapbook and stories from *Owl* magazine, we'd glue those in, too. I remember the glue bottle, with its little rubber pig snout. Granny was a great one for scrapbooks."

I wanted to say, I had to be away, I had to have a job, but I didn't have the heart to reply. I realized that by not being with Lara more in those formative years, I had missed as much as she, perhaps more. Put that in your scrapbook, I felt like saying. Put in a mother's loss and sorrow. "She loved making notes and writing diaries and taking pictures," I said instead.

We were nearing the end of the hall, a shadowy hall lit by low-wattage wall fixtures. My head was down, my eyes distractedly following the carpet pattern. I could feel Lara's presence beside me. I had a strange sensation. Perhaps it had to do with the subject of our conversation or perhaps with the situation we had just left and the whole large subject of life and death, but it seemed to me that at my side were my mother and father, my sisters, my aunts and uncles and cousins and grandparents, even my children and grandchildren, all the people who had marched through my history and were no more, all the people who might be in my future that I could not know. Lara embodied all of my past and all of my future rolled into one, she was the keeper of our family's past and future. Every family has its own particular narrative, I figured, its characters, its plots, the values and traditions by which it propels itself. Every family has what you might call its theme. Lucky families have a member who will keep the story and carry it forward.

Immediately, I rejected such a thought. I did not want any child of mine to have the responsibility of such a task. I did not want any child of mine to suffer the pain of digging and probing and shining a searchlight into dark corners better left undisturbed. I did not want any child of mine to know the desolation of isolation and separation from the real world that such a task demands.

As we rounded the corner at the end of the hall, I raised my head, suddenly. My eyes caught a quick movement, a glimpse of something, not even some thing, a shadow of a thing, disappearing through the stairwell exit door. It was the same mysterious thing or no thing I had seen before, that blur around a corner when I opened my apartment door, that mote in the corner of my eye as I waited for the elevator. Someone needed to tell her to leave Fred alone and I was just the person to do it. I hurried my footsteps.

"Where are you going?" called Lara, who had headed in the direction of the elevators.

"I'm going to take the stairs."

"Why are you running?"

I plunged through the heavy fire door. I leaned over the stairwell. The figure was below us by about two floors. It had long black hair, long legs, a mini skirt and red high heels. She glanced up at me then scurried down the remainder of that section of stairs and disappeared through the exit door into the corridor.

I hurled myself down the stairs. Lara was close behind.

By the time we followed Legs into the corridor, there was no sign of her. I headed for the elevator.

"Where are you going now?" queried Lara.

"Lobby," I explained, pushing the down button.

"Why? Why are you acting so strangely? Who is that woman?"

"That's what I'd like to know." We stepped through the open door of the elevator that had arrived surprisingly quickly. I pressed the 'L'.

"If we're going down to the lobby," said Lara, "you'd better do something with that gun."

I looked down. Sure enough, it was still in my hand. I had on a grey lounging outfit that was, in fact, supposed to be worn as hiking underwear, so didn't have pockets. I stuck the gun up under my shirt and crossed my arms beneath it to hold it there. Luckily, I was also wearing a bulky cardigan.

In the lobby, I accosted Schmidt who was sitting in her box reading a paperback. She knew nothing. She had seen nothing.

I went through the glass doors that separated the foyer from the entrance chamber. I went through the outer door onto the street. I looked both ways through the clarity of cold. Nothing. Perhaps she was still in the building. I turned back in.

Uranus, planet of the unpredictable, must surely have been changing signs. For, as Lara and I were about to step on to the elevator who should I bump into, literally, but that solid presence complete with overcoat and hat that was Sergeant Rock.

Since we were directly in line with the elevator door closing behind him, Rock, in stepping forward into the lobby, moved me with him. We might have been practicing a dance step. Conscious of the gun which I could feel slipping, I hugged myself. "I thought your case was closed," was the first thing that came to my mind. Then, to fill what to me was an awkward silence, I blathered on. "You haven't left any messages lately." As I said the words, I realized that I missed those cryptic codings. I missed that steady voice coming from out of nowhere. I missed the firm reality of the man. I missed his absent arm.

"I'm looking for you." As usual, the sergeant was in command, his eyes steady rocks against my shifty ones. But there was also a new strange look in his eye. When we had been pressed together, he must have felt the steel in my bosom. What was the penalty for carrying a concealed weapon?

"Why? What have I done?"

"I need to talk to you."

"But..." For a wild moment, I wondered if, after we'd left, Aunt Olive had pulled the trigger. Then I remembered that she didn't have the gun. Then I thought that someone might have heard the commotion and called the police. Could Aunt Olive be charged? Attempted murder? Threatening murder?

Just then Rock's cell rang and he had to rush off to another crime scene. "I'll catch you later," he promised in what seemed to me an ominous tone.

"Who's that?" said Lara as we watched him stride out through the glass doors.

"Sergeant Rock." We stepped onto the elevator. "He was investigating that murder that happened just below me."

"Here we go again." Lara pushed number twelve.

"What's that supposed to mean?"

"He has only one arm."

"So?"

"You can't resist men who have only one arm."

"How do you know that?"

"You'd be surprised what I know," she said.

As the elevator began its ascent, one question was dominant in my mind. Why had Rock been hanging around the coffee shop that day? If the case was closed, why was he in our building?

"He has the hots for you," Lara murmured close in my ear.

"Don't be silly," I said.

"Why else would he still be hanging around?

I looked at her quickly. "How do you know he's been hanging around?"

"I see him a lot. In the foyer and the halls."

"Really?" I wasn't imagining it then. My weird thoughts were being corroborated by a reliable narrator. "I've never seen the man without his hat on," I said.

"So?"

"So if he wanted to get close he'd take off his hat."

But Lara was already dreaming the story. "The one-armed bandit who stole my heart." I looked at her in amazement. An enigmatic smile curved her lovely lips as she watched the lighted numbers announce our ascension. "I'm beginning to feel weird," she went on. "Palpitations, cold sweat, abnormal breathing. It's like being in love, isn't it?"

My amazement turned to horror. "Sounds more like the flu," was what I said. Has she caught it from Harry? was what I thought.

The instant we opened the door to the apartment, I knew that everything was different. The tapping had stopped. Before me was a light bright space. The curtain was rent, so to speak. It had disappeared; it was no more. A golden sun streamed unfettered through the plate glass, enriching the white interior to rich cream, intensifying the splashes of colour in the room, the whole reflected and magnified in the mirror tiles.

"Since when has the sun been shining?" I asked anyone who was listening.

"Since this morning," answered Lara. "It's March 21st, the first day of spring."

Winter was officially over. A heavy weight dropped suddenly from my shoulders – the weight of snow, the weight of white, the weight of nothing.

We found Gully in the kitchen, turning from the fridge, hands and arms laden, looking like a man who has just come out of solitary. Two months previous he had been skin and bones. Since then he'd lost weight. His facial hair had taken over his face. His voice was that of one who has not spoken much for a long time. "I'm gonna make myself the biggest goddamn sandwich you ever saw," he grimaced from ear to ear. "I'm gonna drink a gallon of *fresh hot* coffee. I'm gonna trim the shrubbery on this old mug."

"You mean..." I started.

"It's finished," he exulted.

With that, Gully joyfully started smearing mayonnaise on bread.

12.

RAVAGED TIME/HOARDING BODIES/*medicated zombies/ trudge the pavement/through exhaust/clouds/they come to collect her/her meagre luggage...*

Shards/brain/bottle/broken in the gut/shattered brains beneath the bridge//infirm backs bent beneath the mercenary yoke/ submissive they crawl/to river caves/numb in subservience....

I could hear the sound of soft snoring. I realized it was me. With an effort, I pulled myself up and out of a blessed state of unconsciousness. A young lady had taken the podium. I forced myself to listen to the words and to try and comprehend them.

As planets in the sky/stay the same distance always/or crustaceans at the bottom of the sea/you and me...

...or tongue/leaves its strip of flesh/fleck of blood on cold steel...

...she scoops the ravaged air with her twisted tongue...

The young lady sat down. The tall young man with the fantastic black curly hair framing his thin face replaced her. He thanked the young lady and announced again how wonderful it was to see everyone out and introduced the next reader, a young poet who unabashedly stated that he liked to have a bit of fun.

Rooster in the barnyard/pecker in the dirt/rooster in the roaster...

Then we had a middle-aged lady with *Sonatina*, which went something like this. *Cold winter morning static/pierces/ world noise glooms/descends/in the wakewarm darkness/i touch your breathing skin/revenant of love...*

Zzzzz-zzzzz. I was off again.

Lara, who was sitting beside me, jabbed me in the ribs. I looked quickly toward the podium where Rowlf was fitting his guitar over his shoulder. Rowlf's hair was still chartreuse and green and there was more of it. I swear it stood six inches up from his head, in spikes like stalagmites. Around his forehead was a glittery head-band, coiling up his arm tattoos were coppery bracelets. A torn muscle shirt revealed his muscle. I was surprised to learn that he did, indeed, have well-defined pecs and biceps. Baggy pants slung low revealed the band of his jockey shorts and a trim midsection exhibiting further body piercings. He shared the stage with two other young men, similarly decked out and displaying their individual charms.

I was suddenly wide awake.

"Isn't he beautiful?" gushed Lara.

"I... "

Shhh," said Lara, "they're starting."

I understood then why Lara had dragged me out to this poetry reading on a cold winter night that was supposed to be spring.

"Want to come with me to a reading?" she had asked at the dinner table. The two of us were dining alone.

"No," I had answered. "I don't ever want to go to another poetry reading. In my entire life, ever again," I added for good measure.

"You used to go to them all the time," she accused. "You were always going to readings, driving into the city from the ranch."

I could have said, "I did not go to them all the time." Then she would have said the equivalent of "did too" and I would have said the equivalent of "did not" and the exchange would have quickly deteriorated into that of three-year-olds. I did not want to push it. We had been getting along lately. The incident with Aunt Olive and the gun seemed to have given her pause for thought, perhaps given her a clue to adult life.

What I said was, "That's why I don't want to ever darken the door of a poetry reading venue again. Been there, done that."

"You took Rowlf to one."

"That was when I was trying to help him. That was when he was going to write the Great Canadian Novel."

"He's still writing. Just different material."

I did not want to encourage a lengthy exposition of what Rowlf was writing, or even what he was doing these days. I took a large forkful of Lara's lasagna – lasagna had been her specialty at the commune. She had insisted on 'doing' dinner.

"Nothing wrong between you two is there?" I asked, trying to make my voice offhand. "I mean, he seems to be away a lot lately."

"Don't get your hopes up. We're doing just fine. He's busy, that's all."

"I don't suppose he has a job," I ventured.

"In the evening?"

"There are evening jobs. Bartender? Bus driver?"

"No, mother, he is not employed as a bus driver. He has a master's degree, remember?"

I could have wept for her naivety.

We both gummed the pasta a moment in silence. "Well?" she asked.

"Well what?"

"Are you going with me or not?"

"Not," I shot back.

Her face took on its fifteen-year-old look. "You never do anything with me. Daddy spends more time with me than you do, even when he was desperately trying to finish his novel in the time constraints you laid on him."

"Well, where is this 'Daddy'? He could accompany you to the reading."

"He's out, having a good time I hope. He's exhausted after

what you put him through. Six weeks to write a novel! And all your rules and restrictions. You'd think your room was some holy sanctuary, the way you have a bird if anyone even gets close to your door."

We had been getting along so well lately. I remembered that she always could be quite pleasant when she was getting her way. That was when I had a jolting turn of thought, so astounding as to be labelled an epiphany. *Why not give it to her? Why NOT give it to her? If it makes her happy. If it's no skin off your arse. And even if it is. One of us has to grow up, which generally means giving in.* And maybe she was right. Maybe we had not done things together like other mothers and daughters do. I had always considered that our family was populated by independent personalities who liked to pursue their individual interests. Long ago, I decided that there was nothing wrong with going our own separate ways together. But maybe Lara had wanted something different.

"When do we have to be there?" I asked.

Chicks a nickin oka muga, fucka tooa tooa tooa, chucka tooa oda boda, oochalame ooch a ooch a, fucka oocha cham a looi, doozi fizzle fuck televizzle sheeet man, fuck off the fuckin hizzle fo shizzle...

"What is it?" I was awestruck.

"Hip hop, isn't it great?"

"It *does* make unique use of the English language."

"A new way of saying things," agreed Lara. "And what about the rhythm?"

"It is kind of amazing," I agreed.

"And isn't *he* great? You get all the credit."

"Me?"

"That poetry reading you took him to. That inspired him. To take language to a new level. Combine it with rhythm. Make it exciting and contemporary. Shhhh."

We were in the front row. I tried to listen. I understood about thirty percent of what Rowlf was saying since every third word was the *f* one expressed with emphasis. Lara explained to me later that to get anywhere in music these days you have to use bad language. I had to admit that the beat was hypnotic – precise, catchy, relentless. The two on backup did percussion and guitar as well as harmony. The form was a combination of spoken word and music.

On the next number, I watched Rowlf's tongue in fascination, and gradually more words made themselves known.

...cold camphor travel my veins/think you gonna cure me/treat my pain and fever/with your coooool rush?/where you come from camphor/you come from that upside down place/that head-standing place/with your scent of herbs/ strong and weedy/your taste like bitter/waste places?//what you gonna do camphor/you gonna hollow me out?/replace all that coagulated blood/with your cleeeean jet stream/you gonna make the mind snap snap/make the body snap snap/ you gonna poison me camphor?/you gonna explode me/with your white flowers?

Or something like it, edited for expletives.

But, apparently, what Rowlf was really into was social protest, which as Lara explained later fit in with his sociology sensibility. He finished with a lengthy number, explaining that he was still working on it but he wanted to try it out: *sittin on yer fat ass livin in the city/big mcmansion my yore pretty/matchin SUVs triple garage/dog kid and nanny you ever pause/to think of yer neighbour who's down in the hood/or living in the sticks where life ain't good/or though he don't own it the one on the land/growin shit like coffee and ain't it grand/earnin a buck a day so you can juice up/on yer fancy latte in a paper cup (it's organic too)/hey diddle dumb fuck man that's you...*

I looked around me. The crowd that had been at the reading had pretty much taken over one end of Earl's. A couple of young waiters who had thought that they were going to have an easy shift on a stormy mid week night, were skating from table to table with trays full of drinks and arms full of nachos and chicken wings. All around me people were talking in excited tones. Some were shouting. There was much laughter. These young people, these young poets, and a few oldies like myself, were having a good time. They so loved being together, to be around other people who had the same values and interests and hopes and dreams, they didn't want to go home. This is wonderful, I thought. This is the way life should be when you're young. Not only when you're young, a small voice inside me nagged. This is the way life should be at any age. It's good to be where there are people, laughter, life. What am I doing holed up in my apartment fucking flabby old Harry?

I had another revelation: so what if a lot of them wrote bad poetry? Some of them would develop into better poets, all they needed was time. Most of them would become engineers or insurance adjustors or homemakers and never write another poetic line. They would embrace real life without regret, because they had had their time of flying outside the cage. Most people voluntarily exchanged the loneliness of flight for the chaos of relationships. After all the weeping and sighing over lost loves and longing for future ones, all that morbidity of alienation and bitterness of betrayal, most people settled down with a house and kids. Such people were the backbone of community; they were the ones who continued the human race. It was an heroic act, taking up the challenge of the normal. The ones who insisted on staying outside making lonely circles in the thin air were the aberrations, necessary for balance, but still aberrations.

My eyes rounded the noisy, raucous room and came back to Lara at my side. Her eyes were glued to Rowlf who was at another table, such naked love in them that I was frightened for her. Only disillusionment could follow. Well, that was something they would have to work out for themselves, the transition from early lovers to familiar lovers. Every couple had to. And sitting there amongst those young people that evening, I had the uplifting thought that some people did manage it. Some people managed to grow with each other, to help each other develop into human beings. Some people managed love.

Lara swung her head and caught me looking at her looking at Rowlf.

"That's the fellow with the basement," she said, nodding her head toward a member of his band. "Where they rehearse. Where he's been spending so much time lately."

I ordered more wine, one red, one white, and thought how many girls model themselves after their mothers. I thought how Lara had totally rejected the model.

How does it happen? my thoughts rambled on. You have a child, you hold her inside your body, she travels the tunnel of your bones, you hold your darling baby in your arms, you love her so much, you're so happy. In spite of all the other shit that might be happening in your life, you're happy. How can you possibly end up being strangers?

I thought how I had to give up my defensive attitude because it didn't get me anywhere. Lara would not truly alter her judgment of me until she was middle-aged. Not until she had lived more of life would she admit such evidence as the anguish of unfulfilled desire, or the attempt, however futile, of the attainment of a dream. Not until she was brought to her knees by life, which I did not wish for her but knew was inevitable, would she have compassion for the human condition as embodied in her mother.

"You kept everything. You never threw anything out. The house was always such a mess because you were writing." Lara had turned to me and was lifting her fresh glass of wine.

I raised my glass. "Other people's things. My mother and grandmother, my sister too, the one who died, and then you kids, when you left home, you all left it for me to take care of. I felt a responsibility to keep everything." It was people I let slip through the cracks. But I kept the thought to myself. I didn't want to spoil the evening.

"When I went away to university, I left a whole closet full of things."

"I still have them."

"Granny's tea set. That she gave me when I graduated from high school. And an embroidered cloth that had been in her hope chest."

"I still have that, too. It's in a box in my closet. After the wedding, when you have a place for it, you can take it."

"What I'm finding in your trunk. It blows my mind."

"A family's history."

"The usual confused mess. A jumble. No order. It needs sorting, but at least you kept it."

I kept my mouth shut. I didn't want to put my foot in it and spoil one of those rare and wonderful moments when a child of yours admits that you did something right.

"The kitchen table," Lara went on. "I'll never forget the kitchen table at the ranch. Papers, books, magazines, everything ended up on the kitchen table, along with plates crusted with food, coffee cups, a fossilized sandwich wrapped in wax paper that'd been in someone's lunch bucket, homework..."

"And don't forget pages of my thesis..."

"...elastic bands and paper clips and crumbs and dried food from bygone meals."

"Remember the twist tie?" I asked.

At that we began to laugh. We laughed until our sides ached. It had happened during my bread-making period. I used to clear myself a spot on the table to knead the dough. Once, by error, a twist tie escaped from the mess and got itself mixed in with the bread.

"And Richard," Lara gasped, "of all people to get it in his piece. He was so finicky about food, he was so totally spoiled. I'll never forget the look on his face." At that she gasped again and bent over.

"He didn't eat bread for weeks," I shrieked.

"And the way you kept setting off the fire alarm!" wailed Lara.

"Because of grease build-up in the oven," I shouted.

On it went. The list of my housekeeping and cooking errors, with which I had so often flagellated myself over the years, now seemed screamingly funny. And while the errors that led me to the mountain were more serious, they, too, were me. Careless, that was me, who I was, the root cause of both trivial and serious mistakes. But they were all done, the whole mess that was my life was done. I accepted my grave and serious faults. Looking at Lara's laughing face, for the first time, I was truly glad that I had been called back from the mountain. And it occurred to me – Lara was the reason. Not Harry. Lara.

"All of us running around like chickens with our heads off…" Tears were streaming down her cheeks. "Dad, calmly dealing with your chaos. With that resigned look on his face."

"Maybe," I said when I could regain sensible speech, "maybe that's why I became obsessed with order. Maybe that's why I married my last husband. He was such a neat compact man, making those clean lines in clean snow. When I moved into the condo, I was determined to keep chaos out of my life. I put my papers, notes, unfinished manuscripts in neat boxes and neatly labelled them." I reflected a moment. "My life is in those boxes." After three glasses of wine, I was getting a little sloppy.

Through the smoke haze of the bar and the wine haze of my vision I could see Lara's bright eyes. They had a wary look, wary and watchful, maybe even a little fearful. It was the look a person gets when they think you're going to ask them to do something they don't want to do. But Lara didn't need to worry. I wasn't going to ask it of her. My writing was not my children's responsibility.

I recalled the sensation I'd had in the shadowy hallway, the conviction that Lara was the keeper of our family story, that she was the one destined to carry it forward into the future. But I envisioned her as the keeper of scrapbooks, not bound volumes. I did not want her to become involved with Harry, capricious, perfidious, inconstant Harry. She would have to be stronger than me to put up with his comings and goings. She would have to be stronger than me.

So we left it at that.

Sitting there with Lara, feeling close and connected, it was a good moment.

13.

———⚬⚬⚬———

THE NEXT MORNING I SLEPT IN – not so much slept in as snoozed in. I awoke at my usual five-thirty, curled around Harry as I was wont to do these days, then for a couple of hours drifted between the various stages of consciousness and unconsciousness, running my new novel on the video of my mind, letting the creative vibes reverberate.

I must have again fallen into a deep sleep because the next thing I knew someone was buzzing my apartment, insistently, and no one was answering it. I peered at the red numbers on my clock radio. Nine-thirty. Where were Lara or Rowlf, or even Gully? Although, Gully, with some fairly strongly voiced suggestions from me, should have been out scouting new digs.

I looked in the other direction. Was Harry sleeping or merely dozing? What part of the cycle of falling and rising, sinking into the coma of self, surfacing into the real world, was he in?

The buzzer sounded again.

Oh hell, I thought. Someone must have forgotten a key. I lurched out of bed and into the living room and picked up the intercom. "Purolit Courier Delivery," it was a male voice.

"Buzz the concierge," I said. "She'll take it for you."

"I have special instructions," said the voice. "To place this in the hands of a Mr..., the voice paused, "Gully Jillson."

"He isn't here. Go away." That was what I opened my mouth to say. What came out was, "Who's it from?"

After another moment of silence, "I can't make it out. It's a large envelope ... heavy, like a book or something."

"I'm Mrs. Gully Jillson," I said. "Come on up." I pressed the buzzer. I waited.

It turned out to be a legitimate delivery and not a con man or rapist. In fact, the young man seemed to have some fear about his own well-being. After an alarming glance at my attire – it was only then I realized that I was still in my nightgown, although it was flannel and quite proper in that sense – he hesitantly surrendered package and delivery slip into my hands. "I don't know if I'm supposed to do this," he had a worried look on his face.

"It's all right. I'll make sure he gets it," I assured, signing the form in a series of illegible squiggles supposedly reading, Mrs. Gully Jillson. Closing and locking the door, I carried the large white cardboard envelope into the bedroom. I looked at it for several minutes. There was no question of me not opening it, especially when I made out *Knopf* in the *From* square. I pulled the tab on the outer envelope. I lifted out a thick brown envelope. I tore the top of that open. I pulled out a sheaf of white paper upon which appeared black marks. When the black marks took form, they became, *The Long White Sickness*. A covering letter from a senior editor went like this:

Hey Gully, great stuff.

Since we're old friends I shifted your manuscript to the top of my reading list. I'm pleased to report I found the material so intriguing, I read the entire work in a night, kept me up 'til three in the morning ... thanks for thinking of us with this your first novel in a long time ... it'll do the press proud ... few minor edits...

In town next week ... let's get together over a coffee ... discuss contract....

I slowly sank down on the bed beside the comatose Harry and started to read: *This is my official autobiography, a scorching tale of desire and betrayal.*

I read a few more paragraphs, although I didn't need to. I could anticipate each sentence, each phrase, each word. I skimmed through several pages. I noted the number of pages, 250. I noted the last page where it said in large letters, THE END. Gully had beat me to it again. I was only on page 112 of my copy and even those pages were bashed out first draft. He had written all this while I had been having coffee with Aunt Olive, stalking Legs and looking for the neighbour's cat.

I felt nothing. I was in a state of cold shock. I kept reading. I couldn't stop. I was dying to know what was in the remaining pages. I was dying to know the end.

But I didn't get that far before I heard a key in the lock.

The sound was like a slap in the face, bringing me out of shock and escalating me into fury. My temperature rose alarmingly. That this man had appropriated my story once again was bad enough, but this time he had also appropriated my life. I felt prickly sensations along my whole body, my legs, my arms. I was at the boil. Calm down, I told myself, but I didn't pay attention to myself.

I heard the apartment door open and close. I heard Gully's dry smoker's cough. "Come in here," I called. I stood up, in battle stance.

Then came a butter-wouldn't-melt-in-his-mouth "What?"

Oh, the bastard.

"Come in here," I repeated.

"Your bedroom's off limits remember?" The voice was closer to my door.

"Obviously, you didn't remember."

Silence. I knew what was going through his head ... oh, oh, she found out, she's on the war path, think up a good story, quick.

"You may as well come in," I said. "You're quite familiar with my room, having spent the winter in here."

Nothing. I was afraid he might sneak back out of the apartment and I wouldn't get my chance at him. "Come in here this minute," I demanded in my most threatening, most authoritative voice, the one I used to use on the kids.

The door, which was partially open, opened farther, slowly, cautiously. Gully stepped in. He saw immediately what had happened, the courier envelope, his manuscript strewn across my bed. At least he had the grace not to appear surprised at the presence of Harry who remained impassive and neutral throughout the scene that followed.

"You knew Harry was here all along didn't you?" I accused. "I suppose you got some cute little nurse to give you the information." But in speaking the words, I knew that wasn't the way he had done it. I saw the scene on the running video of my mind. He had called a red alert in one of the wards, which had provided him with the opportunity to slink behind the counter and look up Harry's records. "That's why you showed up at my door," I rushed on. "And then you stole my keys out of my purse, which I admit I shouldn't have left lying around, but who would think that when, out of the goodness of your heart, you let a near-perfect stranger share your abode, he will then take advantage of you by raiding your purse! You had copies made. Then every time you had a chance, when I was at Aunt Olive's, when I was out getting groceries for *you*, you came in here and talked with Harry. You read my computer files, you read my notes. You sat on *my* bed!

"And you *listened*! You listened to my private conversations with Lara and Aunt Olive and Sergeant Rock. You *eavesdropped!*"

He looked at me with alarm. His eyes behind his glasses, stylish author glasses – when had he gotten new glasses? – took me in from top to bottom. He must have seen Lady Macbeth in the dagger scene, face contorted, hair wild, nightdress crumpled, eyes blazing with madness. But he wasn't afraid. Instead, he was confident and strong. Thanks to me, he was looking good, like a chipmunk with cheeks full of nuts, the result of two weeks of unrestrained eating. Gone was the uncouth leprechaun who had slipped into my apartment last January, gone was the burnt-out case who had emerged from solitary. In its place stood the impersonation of a successful writer, complete with tweed jacket with leather patches on the elbows. All he needed was the pipe and his image could be transferred onto the back cover of his next book, my book.

I knew Gully so well. I knew that his mind would be bubbling with ideas and twisting with trickery, figuring how he could get out of this. Remorse or regret would not be an issue. He would think himself fully justified in writing the story that I would never get written. He would think that he had not had a choice, that he'd had to do what he had done. He had received encouragement and instruction from Harry. It was his job, his responsibility, to do something with that help.

"How did you get it out of him?" I lowered my voice to a hard, cold rage. More than anything else, this plunged me into despair – Harry had talked to Gully while refusing to talk to me.

"I didn't *get it out of him*, as you put it. It was here in this room, in the air, in his breathing. All I had to do was listen. You don't listen, Constance. You never did."

"You need peace and quiet to listen. You need a life without distractions."

"You let yourself be distracted."

"The bottom line is you stole my story. Once again, you stole my story," I could hear my voice rising. "You no-good, low-down sonuvabitching bas..."

He raised his voice to cut mine off. "*Your* story was going nowhere. You were stuck on that mountain. All that prattling about snow, life as a snow pattern, outer landscape paralleling inner landscape or vice versa. Your book read like notes to yourself. It doesn't matter, image and metaphor, who gives a shit? All that anguish of the blank white page. And I did keep some of it. You *could* thank me for that. You were suicidal for Christ's sake. I saved your life. In case you haven't noticed, I worked my ass off for two months to get you off that mountain and then out of your room where, true to form, since you never learn, you let yourself get stuck again, totally bogged down on the homestead. You should be thanking me on bended knee for putting a dip in the long boring prairie road."

"I'm not going to stand here and listen to your inadequate excuses. The fact of the matter is, once again you've ruined my novel. Once again, you've turned a novel about the depths of the human condition into one-dimensional burlesque."

"Once again I've salvaged your mess. I've rescued your novel from the basement of the past and brought it up into the light of present day. I've saved you! You've got your young lovers, you've got your mother/daughter reconciliation, you've got your old lover's triangle. The human dimension. You've got *life* baby. *Real life!* No one wants to read about your sordid non-affair with Harry, your weeping and wailing about his betrayal. Harry betrays everyone. You're old enough to know that."

"The least you could have done was let me have some *good* sex!"

"Hah! Even I am not that good a writer."

I choked on retaliation. I was too busy going beet red from head to toe because of my indiscretion.

"Queen of the Fadeout. That's you. Always was, always will be. You call it your romantic nature. I call it bullshit. Anyway, there's Rock."

"What about Rock?"

"I kept him in the building for you. You would have let him get away."

"I don't need Rock."

"You see? You never learn."

"And while we're on that subject, what about the murder. Talk about a plot line that fizzled out..."

"It ain't over 'til it's over. Somebody famous said that."

"You mean..." I couldn't go on. He was the one with the end

of the story. Not me. Gully. He knew how it had to happen.

When I resumed listening, he was speaking, "...bitter pill that it may be to swallow, you'd never get anything written if it wasn't for me."

"Really?" I found myself saying. "What about my several volumes of poetry?"

"Anybody can write poetry. Hundreds of books of bad poetry get published in this country every year. Everybody wants to express his innermost feelings. Self-indulgent navel gazing, any high school kid can do that. It takes brains and wit and strength and discipline and hard, hard work to write a novel."

That was when the gun leaped into my hand. Aunt Olive's gun. From my night table. All I did was stretch out my arm. I could feel my fingers closing around hard cold steel.

"Now Constance, calm down. Where'd you get that?" Gully's hands were up, palms outward, as if he was fending off blows.

I pointed at the place Gully's heart would have been if he'd had a heart.

"Is that thing loaded? What in Christ are you doing?" At last, Gully's voice sounded worried.

The click of the safety catch being released sounded loud in the room.

"Constance, you're upset now, but you'll regret this later."

He was right. In the words of myself to Aunt Olive, was any man worth it?

"We can work it out. Just hand me the gun."

No, a man was not worth going to jail for. But my novel was. I raised my arm slightly. I braced my right arm with my left.

"I gave you back Lara," he said.

I felt my hand waver again. What about Lara? This would be the end of it between us. Just when we had found each other, we were about to lose each other again. I could have wept.

"Look, we can put your name on the manuscript if it means that much to you."

He was still negotiating when I pulled the trigger and shot
Gully Jillson dead.

14.

———⚬⚬⚬———

I LOOKED AT THE SPRAWLED FIGURE on the carpet. He might have been sleeping except for a red trickle coming out of his head. I felt instant remorse. I had ruined the broadloom. That stain would never come out. I looked at Harry playing dead. What a pair they made. Maybe they deserved each other after all.

I went into the bathroom. I could not believe how composed I felt. Something was finished. The monkey was off my back. I had dealt with Gully, once and for all. I was free. I noticed that I still had the gun in my hand. I set it on the toilet tank.

I washed my hands, using a lot of soap. I'd have to think up a plausible story. Accident? Self-defence? Temporary insanity? It shouldn't be too difficult. It would be my word against a dead man's. I thought of Lara. Sadly.

I combed my hair and brushed my teeth. I washed my face. Coolly, deliberately, I stripped down my nightgown, threw it into the laundry hamper, went into my walk-in closet, found slacks and sweater.

I was pulling the sweater over my head when I heard a commotion in the bedroom, a sort of scuffling, along with grunts and groans. I whipped myself around to the closet door where an astonishing sight met my eyes. There was Legs, hair whirling around her thin face, an attacking dark angel, leaning over Harry, hauling him out of bed, scolding and pummelling him with soft fists, pushing his arms into shirt sleeves, his legs into pant legs. It was not an easy job. He was groggy, like someone who has been drugged and is having a difficult time surfacing. He must have lost a good deal of muscle strength lying in bed those months. It struck me. He'd been shamming the last while. When I had gone out, he had been up exercising. Or raiding the fridge. No wonder he'd had energy for mirth and melancholy.

He was on his feet, he was leaning on Legs, he was moving his feet in a shuffle. While I stood stunned in shock, she found his coat and commenced to drag him out of the apartment. She ignored my presence, even though I had stepped into the room in full view. Then at the bedroom door, she stopped and turned, "He's been faking it," she said, confirming my suspicion. "He won't fake it with me." She had a sharp authoritative voice that matched the efficiency with which she was abducting Harry. It struck me, that voice. I knew it. I knew where I'd heard it before. She was the presence on the elevator saying, "*If* you don't mind..." And before that, she had been a student of mine in a novel writing workshop. She had been writing an historical romance, i.e., bodice ripper. She had been ruthless and determined even then.

"Oh, and," she went on, "you can tell your Missing Person guy he can stop looking."

"You're..."

"Harry's companion on the mountain. You stole him from me. I'm only taking back what's mine."

So saying, she whisked out the bedroom door leaving me dangling like a modifier in a run-on sentence that renders nonsensical the sentence.

They made their way to the apartment door and disappeared into the corridor. I ran after them and came smack up against a large rock, Sergeant Rock, to be exact. His jaw was set and determined, his deep eyes had a purposeful light.

"I've been trying to track you down," he said in his dragnet voice.

My heart sank. The jig was up. But how could he be on my case so soon?

His arm, his good arm, was stretched toward me. "I've written this police detective novel," he said. "Would you mind?" I looked down at the sheaf of white paper in his hand. I looked up. "Take off your hat," I commanded. He looked startled but he complied. It turned out that he had a thick growth of short-cropped curly steel grey hair that would feel just fine in my fingers. Then he smiled. The smile curled up his lips and lit up his eyes. He looked rather impish. "Later," I said, wildly brushing past him.

Ahead of me, making a beeline for the elevator, were those flashing long legs and red heels and Harry regaining strength with every step. I was too late. The doors closed. Legs and Harry disappeared like rats through a rat hole.

In a state of frantic compulsion bordering on insanity, I descended to the parking level, raced to my car, revved up the engine. Out on the street, I spied Legs and Harry in a flaming red sports job backing out of a parking space, Legs at the wheel. She stopped to shift gears, then they were off like a shot, squealing tires, the works. I took off after them, staying as close as I could.

My thoughts were as erratic as my driving. Gully, through the writing community, that cesspool of gossip, must have heard about Legs and Harry. He must have tracked down Legs' address. That night when Schmidt saw him skulking in our building, he wasn't looking for me. He was looking for Legs as a trail to Harry. That must have been the night she faked her death and took Harry off to the mountain. She must have deliberately cut herself, which isn't hard to do as anyone who does any cooking can tell you. She must have smeared the blood around; she must have been the anonymous caller. Gully was casing her joint when he managed to get a smear of blood on his shoe. Then he came up to my apartment and found the brochures and the missing skis. How his thoughts must have whirled then, trying to figure what it was all about. A couple of days later, he read about Harry in the paper. He read about a dead skier. He read about a missing woman on a mountain. He put it all together. When Legs came back from the mountain, he knew that, too. He knew she was in the building looking for Harry. He had to get to Harry before she did. He had to keep her from knowing where Harry was until he was finished his novel.

But why had Legs faked her murder? The answer had to be that she planned for the two of them to disappear together, leaping into the white unknown. And she must have been planning the caper for some time. She had taken the apartment below me nearly three months ago. It must have been coincidence. She could not have known then that Harry would end up with me. She took him out on the mountain. She lost him to the avalanche. Then she had to find him and get him back. Well, she had him. She had won. He'd be sorry. She'd smarten him up all right. No more lying down on the job. She would get what she wanted out of him. She had youth, beauty, strength, energy and, most important of all, time.

Ahead of me, I could see the red car speeding up Fourteenth Street. I was losing ground. Several cars filled the space between us, but red is a good colour to follow. It changed lanes to the left and careened around the bend onto John Laurie Boulevard. I pulled out of my lane, passed a few cars, cut back in. I made the turn just as the light changed to red. They were far ahead, but still in my sights.

Not only was I exceeding the speed limit, but I was passing all the other cars that were exceeding it. Still, Legs and Harry were outdistancing me. I pushed the pedal to the floor. I might have had success but for a huge merging semi I couldn't argue with. He cut in front of me and cut off my view. Another semi was on my left so I couldn't pass. By the time I got out of the tangle of semis the red convertible was nowhere in sight. I thought of Lara and my common sense kicked in. I could not let her find her father's body. I would have to go back and report something. I would figure it out when I got there.

I swung the wheel for a U-turn, then had to stop for a stream of oncoming vehicles. As the cars and trucks whizzed past, I became more and more anxious. I envisioned Lara returning to the apartment. I envisioned her shock, her pain.

A short gap appeared in the long line of traffic. I stepped on the accelerator. My old frog leaped into the eastbound lane. Then it shuddered to a stop, its old regrettable habit.

In a spectacular leap I was airborne. The other car was a large American job. It lifted me up as if I was nothing, lifted me up and flipped me into the air where my old rusted body performed a couple of somersaults. I could only imagine a great crash, flying metal, flying glass, the jolt to my being, like being hit, being hit hard, by someone or something very large and powerful. I can vouch for the fact that you don't know what happened between the time of impact and the time that everything comes to a stop. But while I was up there I did have an instant of time for one sensation, the one I used to have at the start of a magnificent run, the Armageddon Run, for instance, the exhilarating rush you feel as your feet lift free of the earth.

AFTERWORD

———⊙⊙⊙———

CONSTANCE ALWAYS DID TEND TO OVERDRAMATIZE events. Her autobiography is no exception. Some might call the whole thing a figment of her imagination. Some might call it myth making. Some might call it by what it is, out and out lying. And while some of us might feel a little sad at her passing, we shouldn't. She liked to think of herself as the tragic heroine of her own story. And, although I do not wish to disparage her memory, I feel compelled to set the record straight for those of us left behind to bear the brunt of her distorted, might I say perverted, point of view.

First and foremost, I take exception to her accusation that I went soft. She got me when I was in sad disrepair. After all, I nearly died on that mountain. My reputation depends upon my defence of this malicious gossip. I have always prided myself at rising to the occasion when called upon, as a fantastically large number of females could testify. Barbara, for instance, whom you know as Legs, has no complaints in that department. Ah, Barbara! Devoted secretary, editor, and consultant, as well as author of a string of successful bodice rippers, she is the best thing that's happened to me in a long time.

And while we're on the subject of the flesh, I resent the term 'flabby.' She should see me now, frolicking on the beach with Legs, our bronzed bodies glistening under the Mediterranean sun.

For Constance, wrong about so many things, was wrong about my taking pleasure in pain and suffering. If there's any truth at all in that statement, it has to do with landscape and not my intrinsic nature. I'm having a great time taking pleasure here in the sunny climes of the south of France.

Then there's her snivelling about my lack of response over the years. It was not my fault that she lacked in the area of feminine wiles and seduction tactics. Perhaps a man, too, likes to be wooed. Perhaps a man, too, enjoys foreplay. Perhaps a man likes to be pursued. Legs took action. She didn't wait for me to accidentally appear in her path, a helpless victim.

Constance's way was that of damn the torpedoes – no subtlety, no artfulness – jump on and ride the hell out of the poor bastard. Those sponge baths – no lingering touches, no trickling fingers. She treated her horses better. Perhaps she would have gotten more of the response she desired with daily massages and rubdowns and sweet sugar.

As to her other complaints – she calls me unfaithful but she was the one who deserted me. She was the one who turned away and followed the skier. Anyway, I never took vows. I'm fickle, I admit it, a free spirit, always was and always will be. That's my nature. How can I be anything else? She did not own me. I never promised her anything, or anybody else for that matter. My duty in this world is to free people from their inhibitions and thus liberate their creative impulses. Let me say, I had my work cut out with Constance, for I truly believe she was totally lacking in a talent for intimacy.

And why would I be faithful to her? Why her rather than anyone else? Barbara, for instance? Barbara who trundled me off to the mountain for research purposes, who even then was writing the now famous Madeleine and the Mammoth series – a lot of trekking across tundra and the Bering Sea and living in caves and hot sex under the animal skins. When she lost me to the avalanche, she was determined to get me back, even if she had to woo old Fred to do it.

Constance complains that I wouldn't stay out of her life, then complains that I did. Isn't that just like a woman? The idea that for thirty-six years I kept interfering with her is beyond comprehension. She was the one who signed up for my courses, who phoned me in the night. She was the one who ran into me on the mountain, practically skewering my jugular, I might add. I was there first. In any case, I did not put myself in her way. She was the furthest thing from my mind at that moment. I had other interests, mainly Barbara. I know for a fact that at one time Constance stalked me. I kept seeing her in the oddest places, in parking lots, in libraries, once outside my window at midnight, when I was entertaining. No, Constance. Sorry. I always had a bevy of beauties at my command. Perhaps I did drop in on you from time to time. I thought we were friends. Upon occasion, we were close, but I have had close relationships with a great number of people, male and female. Constance made the mistake of wanting to be the only one. Such egoism had to be punished. But not by me. Life itself takes care of that.

I believe Constance was a slow learner. What other explanation is there for her trusting Gully when he had deceived her so thoroughly before. With her experience, she should have known to never trust a writer, just as you would never trust a scorpion. A writer will exploit his own mother to get a good story. Think how many have. She should have understood that there is no justice in the writing life. Even if you embrace the skull of the bull there are no guarantees. That's not my fault. Go to God's complaint department on that one.

As for the others, Aunt Olive and Fred danced contentedly off into their sunset together.

Schmidt still sits and I imagine ever will, as keeper of the gate, so immersed in her whodunits that every Tom, Dick, and Harry can get in or out.

Lara became keeper of her mother's boxes as well as the scrapbooks and photos and diaries of her grandmother. From this rich vein of source, she drew material to become a serious literary writer, carrying forward the story of a place and people. In her first title, *The One-Armed Bandit Who Stole My Heart*, along with depictions of the landscape and its inhabitants, she spins a powerful tale of a woman who falls in love with a mysterious stranger who shows up at the homestead one fine summer day, seemingly needing a job but in reality needing a place to hole up and lick his wounds before he can return to confront his enemies. The strange title, I am told, is appropriate to the theme of the novel which has in a general sense something to do with the presence of absence, a bit esoteric for the general population but well-received by the literary crowd. And while Lara hasn't made any money from her endeavours, luckily Rowlf went on to great fame and fortune as a hip hop performer. His first CD, a significant debut and major hit crashing the top 40, featured the piece he was working on at his first performance, the one in which he managed to skewer the social and political ills of the day. Thanks to the benefits of repetition which a recording allows, it becomes easier to make out the words and I quote an example: *two-hour commute makes you mean/bitch bout the price of gasoline/should put more money into bio fuels/who eats tortillas but a buncha fools/air pollution is a real disaster/need more roads to get home faster/seen the price of corn-fed beef?/gives a workin guy cause for grief/get home late and it's overdone/feed it to the dog do another one (even the dog prefers it rare)/hey diddle dumbfuck that's you there ...*

Gully, as you might have guessed, suffered only a flesh wound. The bullet grazed the side of his face and nipped his ear. Ears bleed something terrible. But, all in all, he came out of the story smelling like a rose. An amazing guy, it's not everyone who can recover from being shot by one of his characters and bounce back to write the end. With the publishing of *Love in a Cold Climate*, which the editors thought a catchier title than *The Long White Sickness*, he reinvented himself as a writer.

He got his groove back and put out volume after volume of bestsellers. I gave him that. And why not? He kept me company during the dark days of a dark winter. He had the courage to write the ending. He allowed me the last word.

And in the end, Gully was the only one who truly understood Constance, how she constantly let herself be distracted, running off here and there, not paying attention. She had to learn one of life's bitter lessons. I'm impartial. I show no favourites. But while faithfulness is not in my nature, neither is betrayal. My lovers, or would-be lovers, betray themselves. I have nothing to do with it. I have no moral code. I whisper to the criminal and the saint alike. My only demand is total loyalty, total focus, while the affair is on. Those ranch days when I would visit Constance, or try to, she was always wiping snotty noses, curing dogs of worms, bandaging horses' legs. No wonder I always went off with someone else. Quite frankly, I got tired of waiting for her to show me some affection. Just as I got tired of her whining about failure. The writing life is a failed life. Every serious writer knows that, knows he has failed to live outside the page. Every serious writer accepts the fact and gets down to work.

For those who might feel a little sad at Constance's demise, there's a rumour, unsubstantiated, that she's alive and well in the Foothills where she's enjoying her grandchildren of which she has several. The same rumour has it that she and Rock faked her death so that she could make a complete and blameless getaway.

Frankly, I don't believe it. If she were alive, she'd be pestering me as she had for thirty-six years. On the other hand, this fellow who's writing the highly successful new series of detective novels in the style of Raymond Chandler – tough, smart-talking, straight guy detective fiction – is a police force retiree. His particular gimmick is a detective with only one arm. His first title, *The Case of the Woman Downstairs*, about double agents and an attempt to sabotage a G-8 Summit meeting, with involvement of political figures and the RCMP, has a variety of plot twists that keep the reader guessing right to the end. He's good, which means he's getting help from someone and it isn't me.

I'm too busy having fun with Barbara and her bodice rippers.

As for Constance, whether she's alive or dead, she is free, free from her hated white, free from me. She has been sprung from jail. If I may be allowed a metaphor, she has been pardoned from what could have been a life sentence. And even though she did not invent us as we might have liked, we wish her well, wherever she may be.

Yours sincerely

Harry Weinstein, reporting from the Riviera

ACKNOWLEDGEMENTS

The Novel Colloquium at The Sage Hill Writing Experience and, once again, Robert Kroetsch, facilitator; the Alberta Foundation for the Arts for providing tuition and travel grant to attend; the Stir Crazy Writers (you know who you are); Barbara Scott, who always sees the potential; family and friends for support and patience and, especially, for poets, who chance the high wire act without a net.

Thanks to Luciana Ricciutelli for her close reading and helpful suggestions. A special thank-you to Lynn Crosbie for kind permission to quote from and paraphrase parts of her article in *The Globe and Mail,* "No happy ending for the literary lush," from which I drew inspiration and a title.

Photo courtesy of Jon Hirst

Cecelia Frey was born in northern Alberta, grew up in Edmonton and now lives in Calgary. She has worked as an editor, teacher, and freelance writer and has for many years been involved in the Calgary literary community. Her short stories and poetry have been published in dozens of literary journals and anthologies as well as being broadcast on CBC radio and performed on the Women's Television Network. Numerous reviews, essays, and articles have appeared in a wide range of publications including newspapers such as *The Globe and Mail* and journals as varied as *Westworld* and *Canadian Literature*. Her last novel, *A Raw Mix of Carelessness and Longing*, was shortlisted for the 2009 Writers Guild of Alberta Fiction Award and she is a three-time recipient of the WGA Short Fiction Award. She has also won awards for play writing.